TWISTED MATRIMONY

ADULTERY

BY: T. ELLE TAYLOR

COMING SOON BY T. ELLE TAYLOR

Twisted Matrimony II: Anguish
Twisted Matrimony III: Absolution
A Family Affair: Veils Lifted
A Family Affair II: Ties That Bind
A Family Affair III: Next of Kin

ISBN: 978-1-952511-13-4

TaylrMad3Publishing, LLC
info@taylrmad3.com

PUBLISHER'S NOTE

DEDICATION

Dedicated to my awesome family and friends. Thank you for your endless amount of support. This body of work would be nothing without the love, support, and encouragement from all of you.

Table of Contents

Prologue

"Beg for mercy," the man growled as he hovered behind Paris's naked body. "Please… please let me go," she pleaded.

She only caught a glimpse of his face before he grabbed her and turned her around to face the curtained window, but she clearly saw his navy-blue uniform. He ripped her camisole from her body the second she turned, and now she stood naked in front of a police officer she wouldn't be able to identify.

He trailed his hand down her back and chuckled when he touched her inner thigh to spread her legs. "You want me," he said in a matter-of-fact tone.

"N-no," she trembled, but he couldn't see the smile on her face. He didn't know that this had been her secret fantasy all along.

"Lie down," he commanded, and she obeyed without hesitation.

One of the springs from the lumpy bed dug into her ribs, but she didn't care because she was distracted by the sound of him unzipping his pants. She shivered in anticipation and spread her legs a little wider, inviting him in.

He put his hands on either side of her hips and yanked her backward and positioned himself between her legs. "Beg for mercy, bitch" he repeated in his gruff voice.

Paris cleared her throat and tried to sound convincing. "I'm begging you, officer, please don't do this to me."

He moaned as though he was getting high off her begging, so she begged some more even though what she wanted was the opposite of her words. Her deepest, darkest fantasy was finally coming true, and she could not torture herself by pretending any longer.

While he moaned and rubbed his hands all over her body, she felt the tip of his manhood lightly graze her vagina and her mind went blank. She thrust her hips backwards and cried out in pleasure when she felt the length of him inside her. He was taken aback and did not realize that she was the initiator, so he thrust himself in her with force until he climaxed.

Paris laid on the bed trying to catch her breath while the officer got dressed. From the tone of his voice, she could tell he was satisfied and proud of what he had just done, thinking he had violated her.

"Keep your head down," he warned when she tried to turn around. "I'll come for you again if you cause trouble for me, so you better keep your mouth shut."

"I'm going to tell the world," she provoked him.

A few seconds of silence passed, making her think he had left, but then she heard his zipper again and bit her lip in anxious anticipation. "Clearly you didn't learn your lesson," he said angrily, and grabbed her violently before thrusting himself into her for a second time.

Paris woke up disoriented in a pool of sweat. It took a couple of blinks and the rubbing of her eyes to realize she was at home in her bed lying next to her husband. As much as she hated to admit it, her heart sank at the realization that her night with that handsome police officer had only been a dream. For a split second, she wished it had been real, but the peaceful face of her sleeping husband filled her mind and heart with instant regret. Nothing could change the reality that her fantasies would only be fulfilled in her dreams.

Chapter 1

"… And he just kept bringing in more files like I ain't got my own work to do, you know?"

Maleek had been talking non-stop about an imaginary co-worker who kept piling his desk with files, but Paris knew it was another cover-up story yet again. She kept a polite smile on her face, but she was seething with anger, as evident by the tight grip she had on the steak knife. Another tell-tale sign that Maleek was lying was his use of the word "ain't." For all the years Paris had known him, Maleek had an impeccable vocabulary. He was a well- educated man who was raised in a good, middle-class home with both parents present.

Basically, he had it all as a black man in America. He took pride in his education and being grammatically correct at all times. As if that wasn't enough, he was well-built, standing over six feet tall with broad shoulders, dark chocolate skin, and a charming smile to seal the deal.

"Are you ready for dessert?" Paris interjected. She couldn't stand another minute of Maleek's voice spewing lie after lie. All she could focus on was the sickeningly sweet fragrance emanating from his shirt. Everyone and their grandmothers knew the scent of Chanel no.5, including Maleek, who suddenly wrinkled his nose and excused himself to wash up, leaving his barely-touched dinner plate.

"Finish up your dinner and go brush your teeth and wash up for bed," she instructed their two children.

As soon as her back was turned, a lone tear escaped her eye, which she discreetly wiped away. He hadn't changed. Maleek had not changed a single bit. All their months of counseling meant nothing to him because he was back to his former ways. It was as if cheating was an extension of his personality, or worse, a string in his DNA.

Paris cleared the table as she focused her mind on thoughts of her children. They were blissfully unaware that their parents' marriage was on the rocks, which Paris was grateful for. If anything, she stayed with Maleek because of the children. It was important to her that their children grew up in a stable home with both parents because that was something she lacked growing up.

Maleek came down to the kitchen after about an hour. As usual, all he had on was a pair of grey sweatpants, which was his version of a thirst trap. He always did this after he cheated, and it disgusted Paris. "Baby, I can't find my red Polo shirt. Did you do the laundry?"

"It's not like you're going to wear a shirt tonight," Paris replied monotonously. Her back was turned to him as she rinsed the dishes, but she could sense his discomfort.

"I need it for tomorrow, actually. I'm playing golf with a potential client." "You're an engineer."

"Yes, but my client wants to play golf." "Maleek... do you even know how to play golf?"

"I can always learn. Where is this coming from? Why does it feel like I'm being interrogated right now?"

"I'm not interrogating you. I'm asking reasonable questions."

"Oh, I see where this is going," he chuckled dryly. "You think I'm cheating again."

"Are you?"

"Of course not! I ain't cheating again baby. Why you always gotta bring that up? I'm a changed man."

"And I am a changed woman. A good and tired changed woman."

Maleek stormed out of the room leaving Paris with a bitter smile on her face. This was her life. Although she hated the reality of her husband's infidelity, she still loved him and wanted their marriage to work regardless of how toxic it had become. Divorce was never an option.

The sad part about the whole situation was that Maleek was a good man. He was a loving, responsible, and kind husband and father. He was the type of person who got along with everyone because of his great personality. Everything about Maleek was perfect. From the outside looking in, he was every woman's dream man, except for his sole weakness, which was cheating.

Truth be told, Paris had noticed his wandering eyes long before they were married.

His cheating ways started back when they were in college just dating. Whenever he encountered a beautiful woman, or even if she was just walking by, his whole body would involuntarily turn in the woman's direction. Had he not been her man she would have found it fascinating because it was almost as if there was an invisible switch that turned him into a Casanova. But it was that very trait that also made Paris fall in love with him. He was not only charming but incredibly irresistible when he put the moves on.

A lump formed in her throat as she reminisced about the first time they made love.

They had only been together for a month, and although she wanted to get to know him better before giving her body to him, she just couldn't resist him that night.

Maleek took her to the rooftop of his apartment building, where he had a set up a mattress under a clear tent with fairy lights all around. He claimed he wanted them to fall asleep under the stars, but Paris knew what he really wanted, which explained the rose petals, champagne, strawberries, and chocolates.

They had sex for the first time that night and it was nothing short of magical. Maleek was a very gentle, attentive, and thorough lover. He made her feel things she had never felt before, and from that point on she was convinced that he was the one for her. No one had ever made her body sing the way he did that night.

Paris finished cleaning the kitchen and made sure she had everything ready for the kids before heading up to bed. Mornings were always hectic in the Johnson household, so she always made sure to prep the night before so things would run a bit smoother in the mornings.

She checked all the doors, shut off all the lights, and headed upstairs to face her husband. Even though they'd had a minor argument, there was no doubt in her mind that he still wanted to have sex. Maleek always felt as though he had to compensate her whenever he stepped out on their marriage, so he'd go out and cheat and come home and seduce her as though he needed to create that balance to ease his conscience.

When she opened the bedroom door, the lights were dimmed, and Maleek was sitting at the edge of the bed with a towel around his waist. Her first instinct was to tell him that she didn't feel like it, but the wetness between her legs proved otherwise. Paris could not resist her husband no matter how much she tried, and that angered her.

"Let me take a shower first," she told him before he could get out a word. "I'll join you."

Maleek followed her into the bathroom and helped her undress. He gently ran his hand down her spine, causing her whole body to heat up with desire. Her mind had already lost the battle against her body so she gave in and allowed him to pleasure her into new heights of ecstasy.

After they showered, Maleek wrapped a towel around her body and scooped her up in his arms bridal style. He gently laid her down on the bed, still completely naked himself, and planted gentle kisses from her feet all the way to her mouth.

"Maleek," she moaned breathlessly with a single tear streaming down her cheek. "I need to get some rest."

"Shh… relax baby. I just want to make you feel good."

After another hour of love-making, Paris was completely spent. Maleek had already passed out from exhaustion, but she stayed up watching him sleep. In moments like these, she was convinced that he was a changed man. He was sound asleep looking every bit the innocent man she thought she'd met all those years ago.

Just as she was about to shut her eyes, Maleek's phone lit up signaling a new text message. Their therapist suggested they share the passwords to their phones to keep each other accountable so she picked up his phone and unlocked it, wondering who was texting her husband at this ungodly hour.

Her breath hitched in her throat. On his screen was a picture of a naked woman with a strawberry between her legs. Another message came in a few seconds later and it was the same woman, but this time there was no strawberry.

Paris took a few deep breaths and put his phone back on the nightstand. She refused to react. She would not let this get to her anymore.

It was evident that Maleek would never change, so getting mad was a waste of time, instead, she was going to get even. All the years of playing the good little housewife were over. She loved Maleek with all her heart, but it was time he got a taste of his own medicine.

The morning was hectic as always, but Paris was smiling brightly as she helped everyone get ready for their day. Strangely, she woke up feeling sexy and empowered, which was a new feeling. She went as far as initiating morning sex with Maleek in which she dominated.

Something inside her had snapped. An awakening had taken place within her soul. All her years of selflessly giving herself to an unfaithful man had led up to this moment. Now, she was going to give herself to all the dark fantasies that had been locked away in the darkest corner of her soul. But first, she had to find a willing subject.

Chapter 2

It was a day like every other. Paris dropped the kids off and thereafter returned home to do her chores. Bake cupcakes for the bake sale, purchase supplies for a school project, do the laundry, make a casserole for one of the ladies in the church, the list went on and on.

As usual, Maleek called in to check on her. It was their daily ritual. In as much as being a housewife made Paris happy, Maleek worried that it was not a fulfilling role for her despite her insistence that it was. The reason Paris quit her full-time job as a graphics designer was because she preferred to take care of her family. She loved the fact that she was always available to witness her children's milestones. Besides, she still worked part-time as a freelancer whenever she felt like it; it was her choice.

"How's it going?" he asked, sounding distracted.

Paris smiled upon hearing her husband's voice. "Just sorting the laundry. Why did you call if you're so busy?"

"I will never be too busy for you, my love."

"I'll remember that. Will you make it home in time for dinner?"

"Uh… I don't think so. I'm swamped. I'm thinking of pulling an all-nighter to catch up. I ain't playin', it's a lot of work."

There it was again. The use of the word ain't. He was lying to her as always. Her face fell imagining her husband in a hotel somewhere with another woman. She continued to play dumb to the endless excuses Maleek came up with to be away from home even though it tore her heart to shreds.

"Oh… I guess I'll see you tomorrow then."

"I love you," he replied cheerfully, but Paris had already ended the call.

Paris let out a piercing scream and ripped Maleek's shirt that she had in her hands and collapsed to the ground in tears. The number of chances she had given him to redeem himself bordered on insanity, and yet he continued to disrespect her and the sanctity of their marriage.

Leaving the dirty laundry on the floor, Paris headed upstairs to take a cold shower to calm herself. She developed anxiety, and an addiction to pornography as a coping mechanism for her PTSD. Each time her mind was littered with visuals of her husband having sex with another woman, she would open her laptop and replace those visuals with her own fantasies. No one was ever home during the day, so she could indulge in her twisted erotic thoughts for as long as she needed to.

After her shower, she sauntered into her room in the black silk robe that made her feel the sexiest and collapsed on the bed with a lazy smile on her face. She closed her eyes and arched her back as she imagined an officer walking into the room in full uniform, slowly taking off his belt and whipping her. With each imaginary stroke, her body convulsed, and she let out an excited shriek.

She spread her legs and trailed her finger from her mouth to her vagina. Her body shuddered as she violently pleasured herself, all the while imagining it being an officer raping her. As vivid as her imagination was, she could never give a face to this nameless officer who paid daily visits to her mind.

The sudden ringing of the doorbell jerked her out of her twisted fantasy, and she scrambled to get decent before bounding down the stairs to see who was at the door. The only person who came by during the day was Monique, but she usually called first.

Chills crawled down her spine when she opened the door and came face to face with a police officer. The man was fine. From his razor-sharp jawline on his light brown skin, down to his bulging biceps, all the way to his thick muscular thighs, everything about him was drool-worthy. Paris crossed her legs tightly together to prevent the moisture from trickling down her leg, which would be evident because her robe fell midway down her thighs.

"Can I help you officer?" she said breathlessly.

"Good day ma'am. We received a report that a scream was heard from this house, is everything alright?"

His velvet baritone voice made her shudder. She held on tightly to the doorknob to maintain her balance because her legs wobbled when he spoke. Lost in her own world, her eyes trailed down his body, purposely ignoring the gold band on his finger, and down to his crotch that was outlined by his tight pants.

"Ma'am?"

"Oh! Sorry, um, yeah, no, everything is fine. I left the TV on too loud while I took a shower."

"Are you sure? May I take a look around?" he asked, not fully convinced.

"Yeah! Come on in. I'm alone all day so I sometimes increase the volume a bit too much to drown out the silence."

After his inspection, the officer was satisfied that she was okay. "There have been a few reports of break-ins in this neighborhood recently, so make sure you keep your doors locked."

"Of course. Thank you, officer."

Paris locked the door after the officer walked out and slid down to the floor in a fit of giggles. Having an officer walk through her house while she was completely naked under her robe was a rush she had never felt before.

The newfound excitement re-energized her and made her forget all about her husband and his cheating ways. Instead, she ran upstairs to grab her phone so she could call Monique and tell her about the sexy officer.

Monique and Paris had been friends for over two decades. They had been through a lot together, including Monique's divorce. Their friendship had persevered against all odds. Monique was one of the handful of people Paris considered as friends. She was loyal to a fault. They agreed to meet up for lunch since it had been a while, so Paris quickly got dressed and left the house.

Paris was the first to arrive so she asked for a more secluded table because she was paranoid that someone who knew her would be close by and eavesdrop on their conversation. Paris was a conservative woman for the most part, so people didn't really know her business, and she wanted to keep it that way.

Half an hour later, and in came Monique with her light waist-length brown locs freshly twisted. She had an eccentric style of dressing that turned heads wherever she went, not to mention her toned body that she got from doing cross-fit. This time she was dressed in tight faux leather stretch pants and a bright red top with a plunging neckline.

"Hey girl!" Monique squealed when she spotted Paris. "You sure took your time," Paris teased.

"You know me. I have to make an entrance."

They ordered their food and waited patiently until the waiter was out of earshot before launching into the gossip which so happened to be the police officer from earlier that day.

Paris gave a vivid description of the man, remembering all the little details such as the color of his eyes and his height.

Monique fanned herself dramatically. "Girl, I would have been all over that man doing gymnastics and everything!"

"You should have seen him, Mo. Mmm, that man was fine! I would have done unspeakable things to him if I wasn't married."

"Well, you do have a pass if ever you decided to get a little somethin' somethin' on the side you know."

"Come on Mo, you know I wouldn't do that.

"That's the problem! Everybody knows you'd never step out on your husband, that's why he keeps dipping his willy in every vagina he finds available."

"Look, I know Maleek has not been faithful all the time but..."

"Sweetheart, everybody knows Maleek can't keep it in his pants," Monique interjected.

"I know that. Trust me, I do. But keeping my family together is more important to me. I don't want my kids growing up in a broken home."

"So, you'd rather be broken as long as Maleek is in the home?"

"I'm not broken, Monique. And you know I wasn't raised that way."

Monique sighed and threw her hands up in surrender. "Fine! You keep lying to yourself, Paris, but one day you'll wake up and realize that you've wasted your life on a man who doesn't deserve it."

"I love him. Regardless of what he does, I love him, and that's enough for me.

Everyone else can call me names or think I'm foolish, but I'm not breaking up my family over something that 80% of men do. Maleek is a good man. This is his only flaw."

"Babe, you have lost your confidence. The sexy and vibrant Paris we knew is not the woman sitting in front of me right now."

"I know. Like I told you last time, I'll get my revenge."

"When, Paris? You've been saying that for years, but you never follow through." "I will. I promise. Please just trust me. I know what I'm doing."

Paris took care of the bill and walked out to her car with a heavy heart. Monique was right. The whole revenge story was one that Paris told every year since her fifth year of marriage, but not once had she followed through and actually done it.

Distracted by her thoughts, Paris didn't realize that she had run a red light until she heard the siren. "Damn it!" she muttered and pulled out her license and registration before the officer reached her car.

"Ma'am, do you realize that you just ran a red light? May I see your license and registration please?"

"I'm sorry officer. I've been a little distracted lately... Hey! You're the officer from this morning."

The officer smiled brightly, revealing his dimples. "Ah, yes! The lady with the loud TV. Are you okay? I don't normally run into people twice in one day."

"I'm fine. I've just been a little stressed out lately. I guess it's finally taking a toll on me."

"Let me drive you home. I don't want you getting into an accident." "I'm fine," she chuckled. "Thank you, officer...?"

"Derrick Brown."

"Thank you, officer Brown."

"That's alright, but you're not off the hook. I'm going to tail to until you get home. I have to do my job right."

"Okay, thank you."

Derrick tapped on her hood twice and walked back to his vehicle. If anything, she was more distracted seeing him in her rearview mirror than she was before. Her palms were sweaty, and her heart was racing just knowing that he was right behind her watching her. She drove slower than usual, but her house was not far away so the thrill ended faster than she would have hoped.

He parked on the street and waited for her to unlock her front door and go inside before he drove off. Paris watched his car disappear and couldn't help but feel as though they were meant to meet. After all the years of having fantasies of a faceless man, he finally manifested. She didn't know how to contact him or how to get close to him, but one thing was for sure, the next time she saw him, she would be ready.

Chapter 3

Life was peaceful; too peaceful. It felt like the calm before a storm. Regardless, Paris decided to stay positive and focus on all the good that was happening in their lives. She took a peek at her husband who was getting ready for work. The kids had asked if they could visit their cousins for a few days. They were on a break from school and claimed there was nothing to do at home, so Paris agreed.

With this new development, she thought it would be a great opportunity to reconnect with her husband. They hadn't been to therapy in weeks due to Maleek's busy schedule, so she wanted to make sure they were still on the same page.

"Since the kids will be away for a few days, why don't we have a little getaway? It's been a while since we spent time together." She suggested when he turned to face her.

"I'm sorry, babe, I have a business trip coming up."

Paris frowned and cocked her head to the side. "What business trip?"

"I told you about it the other day, remember? You probably forgot," Maleek chuckled uncomfortably.

"Maleek, you and I both know that I don't forget such things. When did you tell me about it? And where are you going?"

"Why do I have to explain myself all the time!" Maleek yelled at her for the first time since they got married.

"Why are you raising your voice?"

"Because I'm sick and tired of your shit! You don't trust me. And you never will. Yeah, I messed up, but I've changed, and you're still all up on me about the past like you don't see it. Like I haven't changed anything. Man, I ain't doing this shit no more."

Maleek stormed out of the room and slammed the door behind him. Paris recognized his outburst for what it was; a distraction from what she asked him. She knew him well enough to know that whenever he couldn't come up with a good lie he'd simply deflect until she dropped the subject.

She let out a sigh and went about her business. The kids

missed their cousins so Maleek's sister invited them to come over for a week, and now that Maleek was going to be away, Paris would be spending the week alone.

The sudden isolation felt too overwhelming. Even though she was home alone during the day, there was always a comfort in knowing that her family would return in the evening. Her first thought was to call Monique and plan something for the week, but she didn't want to inconvenience her friend, so she decided to go out for a drive to clear her head.

After half an hour on the road, she came across a diner with an interesting name, so she stopped for lunch. The drive helped quell her anxiety as it had always done. Maleek knew how much she hated being alone, and yet his sexual escapades took precedence over her.

"I'll have your breakfast special and a glass of orange juice, please," Paris told the waitress once she had settled in a booth by the window.

The diner had a classic sixties retro vibe to it that she loved. The red leather seats with white stitching perfectly complimented the off-white walls and black and white flooring. It was the most charming diner she had ever been in. The multi-colored jukebox sat in a corner, filling the room with Elvis Presley tunes.

"We meet again," a baritone voice startled her.

Paris looked up at the smiling face of Officer Derrick Brown. She didn't really believe in fate, but there was no other explanation for them bumping into each other on multiple occasions within a few days.

"If I didn't know better I'd say you're stalking me, officer," she teased.

"I'm a man of the law, Ms. Paris Johnson. I'd never do that." "How do you know my name?"

"What do you mean?"

"My name; I never told you my name. How do you know my name?"

Derrick's eye twitched a couple of times but the smile on his face never wavered. "Remember when I asked for your license and registration? When you ran that red light?"

"Oh yeah! That's right. I'm sorry. It's been a rough morning. By the way I am Mrs. Paris Johnson"

"Mind if I join you, Mrs. Paris Johnson?" "Sure."

The waitress returned and took Derrick's order shortly after.

Strangely enough, she felt an unusual sense of comfort around him. Maybe it was because of her fetish, or maybe it because he came off as a genuinely nice guy.

Derrick had a calming presence. He seemed like the type of person one could stay up chatting all night with. It was weird that Paris felt so safe with this stranger, but she couldn't help it. Although her initial attraction to him was purely physical, she had to admit that she liked his personality.

They stayed at the diner chatting away long after breakfast. The lunch rush was just about to begin but they weren't ready to go their separate ways yet, so Derrick signaled for the waitress and ordered lunch for both him and Paris.

"So your husband is leaving you home alone for a week?" Derrick asked. The genuine concern on his face made Paris smile.

"Yep. I don't know what I'm going to do yet, but I have to find something to keep me busy and out of the house. I can't be home alone."

"I've been assigned to patrol your neighborhood; I can stop by a few times to check on you if you'd like?"

She smiled and took a sip of her water. "Thank you, but I can take care of myself." "I know you can, but I'd feel better knowing you're okay. Besides, it's part of my job."

Her gut told her that what she was about to suggest was a bad idea, but that only made her want it more. "Instead of stopping by to check up on me, how about you come over for dinner instead? I mean, I don't know how your shifts work, or if you're allowed to…"

Derrick crossed his arms and leaned forward across the table and stopped a few inches away from her face. He was so close that she noticed his eyes were actually a pale green and not brown.

"Wow, you have beautiful eyes," she exclaimed. "You have the eyes, the dimples, and the abs, geez. How can one person have it all."

He leaned back and smiled shyly. "Thank you for the compliment. To answer your question, I'd love to have dinner with you. You seem like a good woman."

"I'd like to think I am," she giggled. "Will that not interfere with your work?" "I'm on the day patrol next week so that should be fine. There's no rule that says I can't have dinner with a friend." "Hmm, we're friends now?"

"Well, we might as well be. The universe keeps bringing us together." "I can't argue with that."

Derrick insisted on paying the bill so she let him. What bothered her about their interaction wasn't how sweet he was the whole time, but rather that she didn't think about her husband once. Their marital issues were at the forefront of her mind when she left home that morning, but they had completely faded into the background when Derrick showed up.

In as much as Paris had a burning fantasy of being sexually abused by an officer, she wasn't interested in an emotional connection that would sway her from her marriage. There were several things in life that she was certain about and the one at the very top of that list was that she loved Maleek. She loved him with every fiber of her being.

She and Derrick exchanged numbers before going their separate ways. Their whole interaction bothered her more and more as she drove home. Why was she so comfortable in his presence? Why did she let her guard down and invite him into her home? Why did she give him her number?

The last thing she wanted to be was a cheater like Maleek. Yes, she had mentioned revenge time and time again, but as Monique said, it was not something she physically wanted to do. It was one of those things she said whenever she was hurt or upset, but she didn't actually mean it regardless of what her husband did.

Maleek's car was in the driveway when she returned home that afternoon, which was very unusual. He often got off work in the evening or late at night so this was a first. Paris decided to park on the curb because she'd be going to pick the kids up from school soon.

She jerked to a stop halfway to the front door. The loud moaning could be heard from their front yard. Paris's fist curled around her car key in fury. Her grip was so tight that the key broke the skin. Her rage overshadowed the stinging pain in her hand caused by the open wound.

Paris walked up to the house leaving a trail of blood. Divine intervention kicked in at that moment because Monique suddenly showed up out of nowhere and pulled her away right before she got to the front door.

"Snap out of it, babe. He's not worth it," Monique said repeatedly.

Monique drove Paris to the hospital after seeing the deep wound in her hand. "I think you're going to need stitches," she said to an unresponsive Paris. Seeing the state her friend was in, Monique offered to pick the kids up from school. She asked the doctor not to discharge Paris until she returned.

After dropping the kids off at her house, Monique drove to the Johnson's home. Just as she expected, Maleek was still ravishing the floozy he selfishly brought into their home. She walked into the house without knocking; after all, Maleek didn't deserve any respect.

The sight before her eyes was both disgusting and infuriating. Maleek had his pants around his waist and his secretary bent over in front of him on the dining room table. It was obvious that they stopped by to pick up some documents, judging by all the important looking papers sprawled out all over the table and the floor. What she couldn't understand was why it was so difficult for Maleek to control himself out of respect for his wife and children.

Monique was glad that Paris had not seen what she was witnessing. No one wants to know that the place where they have dinner every night has been defiled. Seeing as they were both too soaked in pleasure to notice her, Monique flexed her arm and tapped Maleek on the shoulder.

As she hoped, he jumped back startled and she socked him in the face, sending him sprawling on the floor. She was satisfied when she saw the blood pouring out of his nose, and then turned her attention to his secretary who was trying to cover up her nakedness and slapped her across the face.

"You both disgust me. You should be ashamed of yourselves," Monique spat out menacingly.

"I… I didn't mean to. It-It just happened. Please don't tell Paris," Maleek sputtered. "Tell Paris?" Monique chuckled humorlessly. "Paris already knows! She probably would have killed you had I not stopped her. Come to think of it, I should have let her do it. The world doesn't need trash like you."

Monique turned and walked out with her head held high, but she was hurting for her friend on the inside. She watched Paris put up with this for many years. Unfortunately, there was nothing she could do besides punching the bastard as long as Paris agreed to put up with his mess.

Chapter 4

Paris was sitting on the couch following Monique's angry pacing with her eyes. It warmed her heart knowing how much her best friend cared about her.

Monique was the definition of ride or die. She was the kind of friend who would show up, no questions asked, if you called her in the morning, middle of the day or night. Paris didn't have other friends, but that didn't matter because Monique was more than enough.

"You need to ice your hand," Paris suggested upon noticing the swelling of Monique's right hand.

"It'll be fine. Maleek is not the first man I've punched in the face."

"Mo, sit down."

"I can't. I'm just so--"

"Monique Raquel Lawrence, sit your ass down right now," Paris said sternly.

Monique threw her hands up and took a seat opposite her friend. "Damn... you look like you're ready to punch me in the face."

Paris rolled her eyes and threw a cushion at her best friend. "You're so silly." "Are you finally going to leave him?" Monique asked once she had calmed down. "You already know the answer to that, Mo."

"Paris-"

"Go home Sista. I'm good." Paris interjected.

"Nope. I'm not letting you stay in this house alone all week. Nah uh."

"Girl, I sent the kids away early and kicked my husband out the house because I need time alone. I need to figure everything out, okay? I love you and I'm grateful for everything, but I need some space."

Monique gave her the side-eye, but Paris knew that the message was received. Besides, Monique had a busy schedule. She had to work twice as hard to live a semi- comfortable life. Although Monique never complained, Paris could see how much she was struggling to keep everything up, so Paris helped her in subtle ways.

The loneliness sunk in the moment Monique walked out the

front door. Paris hated being alone. The silence felt heavy, as though it was ready to swallow her at any given moment.

She left all the lights on when she went to bed that night. The presence of light was the only source of her comfort, but nothing could distract her from the mental images of her husband having sex with another woman on their dinner table.

Monique left out no details when she recounted to Paris what she had seen when she walked into the house. This made Paris all the more grateful that her best friend had stopped her from entering the house.

To think she had almost ended her friendship with Monique a few years prior because Maleek didn't like her, yet Monique was the very person who had kept her sane through all of his mess.

Paris stayed up all night listening to the creaks, squeaks, and other sounds that the house made. No matter how hard she tried, her brain refused to give in and let her sleep. For a split second, she regretted kicking Maleek out of the house, but that thought was trashed faster than it was conceived.

"I guess a hand really is that important," Paris mused as she struggled to undress for her shower the next morning. The doctor warned her not to keep her hand away from water for the first 48 hours so that it wouldn't get infected. Because she had never been wounded before, she didn't realize how difficult it was to get things done, and what made it worse was that she was all alone.

She gave up on trying to shower and decided to make breakfast instead, which also proved to be a difficult task. After multiple attempts to fry an egg with her left hand, she gave up and collapsed on the living room couch feeling defeated. Nothing seemed to be going her way. To make matters worse, her wound began to itch incessantly, but she was instructed to not scratch it.

Feeling overwhelmed and helpless, she burst out sobbing. It felt as though her life was falling apart right in front of her eyes and there was nothing she could do about it. She couldn't make Maleek stop cheating, or her stitches stop itching. Hell, she couldn't even take an ordinary shower!

After she had calmed down a little, she pulled her phone from the pocket of her robe and began to mindlessly scroll through the contacts until she came across the latest entry. "Derrick Brown," she read aloud. Without giving it much thought, she sent him a text message.

Paris: Hey Mr. Officer.

Derrick: I was wondering when I was going to hear from you. Is everything alright?

Paris: No...

Derrick: I'll be right there.

Paris' eyes widened in shock when she reread the messages and realized what was happening. Officer Derrick was coming over and she looked a hot mess. Her hair was tangled like a bird's nest, and all she had on was a hip length camisole and a silk robe. The doorbell rang before she could make it up the stairs and she froze like a deer in headlights.

It had barely been five minutes since Derrick said he'd come over, so how did he get there so fast? Paris breathed out a sigh of relief when she remembered him saying he'd be patrolling her area. She made her way to the door, completely forgetting about her appearance, and opened it to reveal a worried-looking Derrick.

"What happened?" he asked, peeking over her head with his hand on his gun.

"I'm sorry, Derrick," she replied, avoiding his gaze. "I was just feeling overwhelmed. Everything is fine."

He studied her for a moment with a frown on his face. "What happened to your hand?"

"Oh, this? It's nothing. The doctor said it should heal in a week or so." "You didn't answer my question, Paris. What happened to your hand?"

"Can I sit down first? I'm feeling a little lightheaded."

Derrick nodded and walked in after her. He immediately noted the mess in her open plan kitchen. It looked like a tornado had swept through the place.

"I subconsciously dug my car key into my hand when I got home yesterday and heard the sound of my husband pounding his mistress in my dining room."

"What kind of man would cheat on his wife? Much less in their home," Derrick said angrily.

"He's been doing it for years," she shrugged. "The jokes on me because now I'm the one whose hurt and can't even make breakfast or take a shower."

"Say no more," Derrick said, already folding his sleeves. It was only then that Paris realized that he wasn't in uniform. He had his gun and his badge on his belt, but he was dressed in civilian clothing.

Derrick got to work tidying up the place. He told her to sit back and relax while he cleaned and made her breakfast. Normally she would have said no because she hated having strangers invade her personal space, but it felt good to be taken care of for once. She was always the one taking care of everyone else.

After devouring the delicious omelet he prepared for her, Paris got up to take her plate to the kitchen, but he intercepted and gently snatched it out of her hands, causing her to laugh at how ridiculous he was being.

"I'm not completely useless you know," she said cheekily. "I don't doubt that. But let me take care of you."

Somewhere along the way, they had been inching towards each other until there was barely any space left between them. Derrick snaked his hand around her waist ever so slowly with a lazy smile on his face.

"You need a bath," he wrinkled his nose humorously.

Paris gasped and tried to step back but he locked her into his hold. She shut her eyes in embarrassment, but that only made Derrick chuckle.

"I didn't say you stink," he clarified. "I said you need a bath. Come on, I'll help you." "You've done enough already. I don't need your help taking a bath."

"I won't do anything you don't want me to do. Just trust me."

Against her better judgment, she led him up the stairs and into the master bathroom where he immediately began to run her a bath. Her mind was filled with lustful thoughts as she watched his every move. The way his pants tightened around his butt when he bent down to feel the water or the way his muscles flexed with every movement he made; she caught all of it.

"Take off your clothes," he said softly, but there was an undertone of dominance that did not go unnoticed by Paris, and it excited her.

He took slow, calculated steps towards her and untied her robe. "Paris... take off your clothes," he whispered in her ear. The sexual tension between them was palpable, but she wasn't ready to give in just yet.

She raised an eyebrow in defiance, to which he responded with a sigh and took off her robe. His movements were very slow and gentle as though he was handling something precious. He deliberately avoided touching her skin, but that only made her desire for him grow.

When she was completely naked, he picked her up and took her to the tub where he placed her in the middle of the lavender and chamomile scented bubbles and proceeded to bathe her slowly and gently. It was the most intimate act she had ever been involved in. He caressed every part of her body with precision as though he were committing it to memory.

Paris didn't want it to end, but it had gone on so long that the water was almost cold, so she had to get out. He wrapped her in a towel, picked her up, and took her back into the room, laid her across the bed and proceeded to apply body cream all over her body. He went into her walk-in closet to pick out clothes for her and returned with a short red button-up dress that she hadn't worn in ages and a lace thong.

"That's too short," she told him.

"It'll be easy to take off." He said matter-of-factly. "Why would I want to take it off?" she challenged him.

Instead of responding, Derrick knelt at her feet so she could step into the underwear, and pulled it up her bare legs. He stopped mid-thigh and lightly kissed her vagina, causing her body to tremble, and then he pulled the thong all the way up.

"Trust me," he said huskily. "You'll have this dress on the floor sooner than you think."

After dressing her, Derrick took her downstairs and told her to sit on the couch while he made lunch. Having a man cook for her was very exciting. In fact, everything Derrick did excited her. She loved how he took charge and did everything without asking her. Because Maleek was the first man she had ever lived with, she didn't get to experience this kind of treatment.

Yes, Maleek was a good man, but he never did chores or anything else that involved running a household. He worked hard and provided for them, but sometimes she wished he would put a little more effort in other areas.

Watching Derrick work his way around her kitchen made her feel so relaxed and safe that she fell asleep. The comfort in knowing that someone who could protect her was in the house was all her brain needed to finally shut down and let her rest.

Rest was something her life had been missing for a long time, but she hadn't realized it until Derrick showed up and took care of her. Now she understood why her husband and children were so spoiled; she was always available to take care of them. But now, she had someone to take care of her, even if it was only for a day.

Chapter 5

The sun was setting when Paris woke up from her nap. It had been a while since she'd had such a good sleep. A yellow note caught her eye when she got up to stretch. She was about to panic, thinking someone had broken in when she remembered that Derrick came over earlier that morning.

Lunch/Dinner is in the microwave. You looked so peaceful that I couldn't wake you. Rest well my rose, I'll be back later tonight. – Derrick

"My rose," she chuckled. "Who knew that Derrick Brown was a corny guy?"

She went into the kitchen and heated the plate of food without seeing what it was. "Oh my god!" she exclaimed when she saw what was on the plate. Derrick had prepared crispy salmon in a lemon dill pepper sauce. Paris always thought it was cute when men said they could cook because she had never met one who could cook well.

"Who are you, Derrick Brown?" she muttered as she sat down on the couch to eat. Normally she would have sat at the dinner table, but each time she walked past it she saw images of Maleek with an unknown woman getting down and dirty, and it made her want to throw up.

She didn't remember bringing her phone downstairs, but there it was on the couch next to her ringing. "That's odd," she muttered before answering it.

"What would you like for dinner?" Monique asked on the other end of the line. "Hello to you too Monique," Paris scoffed. "I'm already having dinner so don't worry about it.

"Now how on earth did you make dinner with a busted hand? You need to teach me your ways."

"First of all, my hand is not busted," Paris laughed. "Secondly, I've been trying to teach you how to cook for ages."

"And I told you, I don't need that skill to survive as long as I've got this fat ass," Monique popped her lips.

"You're disgusting," Paris shook her head. "How's everything going?"

"Everything is messed up," she sighed. "But I'll tell you all about it when I come over in a few hours."

"You can't come over!"

"What? Why not? It's not like you're finally cheating on your husband." Monique scoffed.

"Of course not," Paris nervously chuckled. "Like I said, I need some time alone, that's all."

"Girl, quit playing. I know you're walking around the house butt naked, and I don't want to see that, so I'll see you in a couple of days then? Let me know if you need anything."

Monique ended the call abruptly without prying, which was very unusual. Paris jumped up and took a peek out the window to prove her suspicion, and right there on the other side of the street was Monique's baby blue Toyota.

Paris smirked and waved when Monique made eye contact, after which her car jerked twice before taking off down the street. The whole thing was comical. Knowing that Monique would pull the same stunt throughout the week, Paris immediately texted Derrick and told him to park in the garage when he came over.

Getting to know Derrick was never her intention, neither was hiding him from her world, and yet there she was doing both those things. Even though her body begged her to fulfill her fantasy, the part of her that loved her family wanted to keep that fantasy locked away, but Derrick was not a man who could be ignored.

He had an air of mystery that intrigued her. There was just something about him that pulled you in involuntarily. It wasn't his good looks or charming personality, but more of an instinct. She instinctually wanted to be close to him from the moment he showed up at her front door a few days prior.

She looked out the window when she heard a car pull in her driveway, and marveled at the Maserati GranCabrio idling in front of her garage. It was only when Derrick's head stuck out the window that she rushed to open the garage. She felt, for the first time since she'd met Derrick, a sense of fear.

The only reason she knew what type of car he was driving was because her husband would not shut up about it. That was Maleek's dream car. She knew everything about that car down to its base price, which made her question how an ordinary police officer could afford one.

Derrick sauntered into the house with a bottle of wine in one hand and a bouquet of calla lilies in another. He looked even more handsome in his white button-down shirt and navy blue slacks. Seeing how relaxed he was in her home set off all the alarms in her head. It was then that she realized that she knew next to nothing about this man and yet she had already been naked in front of him and welcomed him into her home.

He placed the bouquet in her left hand and kissed her on the cheek. "You look rested." "I am… actually, I'm still kind of tired so maybe you should leave."

He took a step back and cocked his head to the side, studying her carefully. Paris fidgeted under his intense gaze but didn't move. It felt like déjà vu.

She wanted to ask him questions, but her brain seemed to have gone offline, so instead, she spun around and headed to the kitchen mumbling something about finding a vase for the flowers.

The distance between them began to clear the fog in her mind, but that only made her panic. It sunk in that she was alone in her home with a stranger and all sorts of scenarios of what he might do to her began to run through her mind. What bothered her more than anything is that she hoped each of them would come true.

Derrick walked up behind her and snaked his arms around her waist. "What's on your mind?"

"Nothing. I just need to put these in water," she said coldly.

He traced the outline of her ear with his tongue, "You're afraid," he said, as though it were a fact.

"Why would I be afraid of you?" she snorted.

As had become his tradition, he didn't reply with words. Instead, his hand went straight to her crotch, and he began to fondle her under her dress. Paris arched her back and leaned her head on his shoulder for support because her legs had gone weak. He started off slow and sensual, but quickly switched it up and became rough and urgent.

"What did I say about this dress?" he grunted in her ear, but Paris was too far gone to reply.

He spun her around and ripped her dress open. The buttons scattered on the kitchen floor, but that's not what had her attention. The look on Derrick's face was both erotic and frightening. His face was set in an animalistic scowl, but his eyes were filled with a burning desire. There was no turning back. Paris no longer cared about being rational or faithful to her husband. All she wanted was to feel Derrick inside of her, but she didn't want him to be gentle.

"You want me, don't you?" he asked her, never once shifting his gaze. "No." she replied flatly.

"You want me to make love to you."

"No."

He spun her around with more force than the first time and pressed himself against her. "Tell me you want me or you will regret it. I always get what I want."

"No," she replied firmly, while seductively rubbing against his bulge. Derrick threw her dress to the ground and bent her over the kitchen counter.

Everything happened so fast that he was inside her before she knew what was happening. Her eyes rolled back as he took her hard and fast without protection. Her fantasy had come true.

When he was done, he took her upstairs and proceeded with round two on her matrimonial bed. The excitement was unlike anything she had ever experienced. Knowing that she had made love to Maleek a countless number of times on that bed only made her desire for Derrick to grow.

Derrick was like an animal. He told her that he wouldn't stop until she had climaxed five times even when she begged for rest. She thought he'd had enough when they went to take a bath, but even then, he placed her on top of him and ordered her to ride him while he kept her hands away from the water.

"How do you feel?" he asked her after her fifth climax, but she couldn't formulate words to describe her euphoria.

"That's my girl," he chuckled and fell asleep with his arm around her.

Paris woke up in Derrick's arms a few hours later and traced faint lines on his bare chest. She couldn't believe what she had done, but she had no regrets. Derrick made her feel like a real woman. She appreciated him wanting to pleasure her more than he wanted her to pleasure him.

Still, a part of her heart broke because she had not kept her vows to Maleek. Even though he didn't know what she had just done, she would know every time she slept in that bed. Instead of worrying about what she could not change, she snuggled closer to Derrick and chose to be grateful that the man lying next to her had brought her fantasies to life. In a way, Derrick had renewed the strength she had lost from fighting for her marriage.

Paris knew that morning would come and Derrick would walk out her door never to return again, but at least she would have the memory of their erotic night together for the rest of her life.

Chapter 6

A month had gone by and life had seemingly gone back to normal. With each passing day, Paris missed her husband all the more and was finally ready to let him come back home. What further influenced her decision were their children who kept asking questions about their father that Paris had no answer to.

Dinner had become an awkward affair with the kids sulking and unresponsive to her table-talk. Their family had been shaken, understandably so, but they were not privy to the real reason their father was not coming home.

"Dad is coming home soon," Paris said as a last-ditch effort to get boost her children's mood.

"Really?" Junior asked. He was a spitting image of his father.

"Really."

As if a switch had been turned on, Junior and Brianna became chatterboxes once again. They had to catch their mother up on everything they hadn't told her in four weeks. It was entertaining, to say the least.

Paris choked up with emotion as she listened to her children babble on about random things that she didn't understand. She was not caught up on the new age lingo so all she had to go by was the smiles on their faces.

The kids were in high spirits the next morning knowing that their father would be coming home. Maleek was many things, but she would never deny that he was an amazing father, and she was willing to allow him back home even if it was solely for that reason.

She picked up her phone to call Maleek to let him know what she had decided but was interrupted by an incoming text message. Her heart began to race when Derrick's name lit her screen up. Up until that day she had done a great job of avoiding him.

Derrick: I need to see you… Please.

Guilt had never been something Paris felt often until her encounter with Derrick. She hated that she had used him to fulfill her desires and then kicked him to the curb to continue living her "perfect" life with her family. It was difficult to get his face out of her mind those first few days, but a month had passed and he had become a distant memory.

Paris remembered how shattered he looked when she told him she couldn't see him again. He begged her over and over to reconsider, stating that he had fallen in love with her, but nothing would change her mind. Maleek was her past, present, and future, regardless of what she had done.

Derrick: Please, Paris.

Out of all his text messages, this was the one that rattled her. Her mind said she should block his number and forget all about him, but her heart said otherwise. Even though she didn't care about him romantically, she couldn't deny that he was a good guy and that she had given him false hope.

Paris: Meet me at the diner in an hour.

It was only right that she gave him the chance to express himself and get closure.

Also, she wanted to make him understand that there was no way she was going to give up her marriage to be with him.

After dropping the kids off at school, Paris drove to the little diner where they had met over a month before. Oddly enough, they never bumped into each other again after spending the night together. It was as if he had disappeared off the face of the earth. The only reminder that he was still alive, and okay was the daily text messages he sent in which he begged to see her.

Paris arrived first and chose the same booth they sat at before. They definitely needed the privacy. The nerves finally kicked in when Derrick walked through the door. He looked more handsome than she remembered.

"Hey," he greeted her, but she didn't miss the sad tone of his voice.

Derrick played with his car keys and kept his eyes down, even when the waiter came to take their order. Anyone could see that he was a broken man. It was only upon closer inspection that Paris noticed the dark circles under his eyes. This was not the sweet and confident officer she had met over a month ago, and it was all her fault.

"Derrick, I'm so sorry," Paris began. "This whole thing is my fault. I had this fantasy for years and… well I used you. There's no excuse for what I did, but I hope you know that it was never my intention to lead you on."

Derrick had a bitter smile on his face but still wouldn't meet her eyes. "You know… you are the first woman I ever fell in love with."

Paris gasped and gripped her seat. "Derrick, I-"

"I don't need you to respond to that," he cut her off. "I just wanted to make you understand why this is so hard for me."

"But we barely know each other." "Is love supposed to make sense?"
"Derrick…"

She forgot what she was about to say when he finally looked at her and she saw the pain he had been hiding. All she wanted to do was wrap her arms around him and tell him it would be okay, but she didn't want to further complicate things.

"How do I get over you? Please tell me what I need to do and I'll do it, Paris. I just don't want to feel this way anymore."

Paris gave in when tears escaped his eyes and stood up to hug him. Derrick's body trembled as he quietly sobbed in her arms, only making her feel guiltier for what she had allowed to happen between them. Her heart went out to him but she still couldn't give him what he wanted.

"I never meant to hurt you," she told him once he had calmed down. "My husband has been cheating on me for years and I let it slide because I love him and because I didn't want to feel like a failure. After we had kids I stayed because I didn't want them to come from a broken home."

"So you've been putting everyone else first?"

"I guess so," she shrugged. "Look, I'm not telling you this so you'll feel sorry for me.
I want you to know that the night we spent together was not a mistake. For once I did something that made me happy and I'm grateful to you for that. I just didn't realize the effect it would have on you and for that I am so sorry, Derrick."

Derrick reached out and wrapped his hand over hers. "I'm sorry, Paris. I was only looking at it from my perspective. You deserve the world."

Although Paris had no intention of having further relations with Derrick, she couldn't deny the electricity that flowed through her body when he touched her and looked at her that way. He was genuinely concerned about her even though he was heartbroken and it warmed her heart.

"Why are you so perfect?" she asked him.

"I'm far from perfect," he deeply sighed. "I'd do anything

for you, Paris. I know I can't be with you, and I accept that, but I'd like to have you in my life if you're okay with that."

"I don't think that's a good idea. I don't want to lead you on, neither do I want to fall into temptation when things get tough with my husband."

"I promise I won't do anything you don't want me to do."

Derrick couldn't keep his food down because he hadn't slept in days, so they left the diner after agreeing to be friends. Truthfully, Paris was skeptical about being friends with a man she had been intimate with, but Derrick was an overall good human being, so she concluded that there was no harm in it.

"Mondays are always dramatic," she mused. She was on her way to Maleek's office to let him know that she was ready to accept him back into their home. When she noticed that the scar on her palm had healed she realized that she could heal from the pain Maleek had caused her with time.

She remembered how her mother would always say, "You don't sell your house just because there's a hole in the roof," which meant you should not give up on a good thing because of one flaw.

"I'm not ready to give up just yet," she sighed when the

company came into view. It had been a while since she had visited him at work. The last time she was there was on his birthday where she arrived wearing a long coat, 6-inch heels, and nothing else. Maleek was into kinky stuff like that. Just the thought of someone walking in on them always turned him on.

Something caught Paris's eye while she was looking for a free space to park in. She could have sworn that was Monique's car parked a few spaces back, but she shrugged it off because Monique had no reason to be there.

"Come to think of it, I haven't seen Monique in a while," she mumbled to herself as she walked into the building.

"Mrs. Johnson!" Alice- the secretary- jumped out of her seat seemingly startled. "Hi Alice," Paris smiled. "How are you doing? It's been a while."

"H-Hi," Alice smiled nervously. "Mr. Johnson is in a meeting."

"That's odd," Paris frowned. "His schedule says he's free."

Paris rummaged through her handbag and pulled out her phone to show Alice. "See, his schedule is synced to my cloud."

"I-it… um."

"It's fine Alice. Take a deep breath; you're not in trouble. I'll just wait for him in his office."

Paris waved at the panicked secretary and strode off in the direction of Maleek's office. There were many times when she had to wait in his office while he attended to other things so this was nothing new to her. She exchanged pleasantries with other employees on the way, but it was becoming annoying because they all seemed to be chattier than she remembered. Finally, after almost twenty minutes of small talk with random people, she made it to Maleek's office.

Paris was startled when the door suddenly swung open and she came face to face with her best friend. "What are you doing here, Monique?"

Chapter 7

Paris recognized the look on Monique's face. It was one she always had when she had done something wrong. Monique was one of those people who wore her emotions on her face, which is why she was a terrible liar, but also why Paris found her to be trustworthy.

"Mo?" Paris snapped her fingers in front of Monique's face.

Monique stared at her shoes and mumbled, "I came to give him a piece of my mind." "Girl, you know you didn't have to do that."

"Yeah… I've got to go. I have an appointment."

Monique squeezed through the small space between Paris and the doorframe and dashed down the hallway and out of sight. "That girl is crazy," Paris chuckled and turned her attention to her husband who was sitting behind his mahogany desk wiping away the beads of sweat on his forehead.

Paris locked the door so they wouldn't be disturbed and sat across from him. It was hard to ignore how panicked and fidgety he was, but Paris chalked it off to him being nervous to see her after so long.

"You can come back home," she said monotonously.

"The kids miss you." "What about you?" Maleek replied shakily.

"What about me?"

"Do you miss me too?"

"Maleek, don't sit there and act like you didn't bring some whore into our home. I may be okay with you coming back home, but that doesn't mean I have forgiven you for what you did."

"I'll get help, babe."

"That's what you always say! How about you actually do it this time?"

"Paris, I love you. I love you more than I have ever loved anyone or anything, and I'm sorry that I keep hurting you. I want to stop-believe me, I do. I've been lying to myself all these years but I now know that it is an addiction and I need to break it. Please don't give up on me."

That was the difference. They loved each other. No matter what Maleek did, Paris could not deny that he loved her. If not for his weakness, he would have been the perfect man, but she had gotten her revenge so she didn't need him to be perfect because neither was she.

Maleek seemed to be a changed man once he came home. He was more attentive than ever and intentional when it came to helping out with the chores. Moreover, he began to attend therapy once again and he joined a sex addiction help group. The results were undeniable. He no longer came home late or spent an excessive amount of time away from Paris. What made her trust him, even more, was that he would call her whenever he was having a hard time controlling himself.

This presented an opportunity for them to spice up their sex life because Paris would drive to wherever he would be and they would make love just to "quench his appetite".

Maleek loved it because he got to reconnect with the love of his life and fulfill his fantasies at the same time.

"How would you feel if we got pregnant again?" Paris asked him one night. They were snuggled on the couch watching a movie after the kids had gone to bed.

"I'd be worried about being outnumbered, but at the same

time, I'd be elated." "Really?"

"Wait… are you pregnant?"

"No! not at all," Paris chuckled. "It's just a thought I've been having since we've been so sexually active lately."

"I must admit, it crossed my mind a few times, but then I remembered you were on birth control."

"Hey, you never told me what Monique said to you that day. It seemed intense." "She threatened to kill me if I continued to hurt you."

"I bet she was graphic with her description of how she'd do it," Paris laughed. Knowing Monique, she probably said some things that would give Maleek nightmares.

This was the life they had in the beginning. It was peaceful and filled with love, honesty, and respect. They were held as the standard for healthy relationships in their community right from the day they got married. People wondered how two black people from broken homes could come together and successfully break free from the trauma of their childhoods.

"Let's host a family fun day!" Paris perked up. It was a tradition they started a few years ago. They were one of the most successful families in their community, so moving to the suburbs felt like they were betraying their roots. Maleek may have had a more financially stable family, but he was still part of the community. After much discussion, they had come up with the idea of a family fun day which became an annual tradition.

The Johnson family sponsored the whole thing. They would set up good food, music, and games at the park, and families would come and enjoy a nice day out without having to worry about the cost. This was one of the things Paris and Maleek always agreed on; giving back to their community.

Maleek said he would pay for the whole event but left the planning to Paris because his job had become more demanding ever since he got a promotion. Paris recruited a few respected ladies from the community to serve on the planning committee and they got the ball rolling.

Word spread fast and soon everyone was excited about the family fun day since they hadn't had one in a while. Everyone was offering to pitch in with whatever they had to offer, and soon it became a grand affair.

"Thank you for doing this dear," Mrs. Goldwin said. "We

thought you had forgotten all about us since we didn't have one last year."

"I'm sorry," Paris apologized sincerely. "So much happened last year that it slipped my mind."

"No need to apologize," Mrs. Adams chimed in. "You and your husband don't have to do this for us, but you do it out of the goodness of your hearts, so we are grateful whenever you can."

"I wasn't saying I'm not grateful Jocelyn," Mrs. Goldwin fired back, having taken it personally.

"Well, you didn't have to make the comment at all Mary," Mrs. Adams retorted.

Soon the two older ladies were in a full-blown argument about who was grateful and who wasn't and had to be separated by the other ladies. As much as Paris didn't like them fighting, she smiled because it felt good to be around people she grew up with even if that meant listening to them bicker.

Remembering her humble beginnings always put things into perspective for Paris. Her husband may have had a better upbringing than she had, but he had still been a victim of a racist system at times and it had scarred him for life, even though he had healed from those incidents.

The energy at the event was electric. The younger people created a makeshift dance floor where they danced until the sun set, while the older generation sat under the shade of the trees sharing stories of their prime years.

Paris smiled brightly when she spotted Maleek and the kids playing flag football with some of the other children. The air was filled with the laughter of people of all ages from different walks of life, which was the best thing about family fun day. No one cared about what you had or didn't have; everyone just focused on having a good time.

Maleek suddenly appeared next to her and wrapped his arm around her waist. "Aren't you going to join in on the festivities?"

She leaned her head on his shoulder and sighed in contentment. "Seeing everyone so happy is enough for me."

"You've always been so selfless," Maleek kissed her forehead. "It's one of the reasons I fell in love with you."

"Oh yeah? What are the other reasons?"

"Um… see, I didn't expect a follow up question." "Hey!" she shoved him away and chuckled.

Maleek wrapped both his arms around her and stared deep into her eyes. "Thank you for coming back to me; more importantly for never giving up on me. I don't deserve you."

Paris swallowed back the guilt that had risen in her chest. She would have loved hearing these words, if her encounter with Derrick hadn't popped in her mind every time Maleek said such wonderful things about her. She wanted to come clean when they reconciled but knowing how much it would hurt him always stopped her from doing so.

"What's on your mind?" Maleek asked due to his wife's prolonged silence. "Nothing, I'm just really happy right now. Being here right now with you, our kids, and our community makes me feel like such a blessed woman."

She laid her head on his chest and said a silent prayer for forgiveness for what she had done. No matter how many times she tried to convince herself that it was okay, she still couldn't forgive herself.

'Is this how Maleek felt every time he was with another woman?'

Maleek shook her out of her thoughts by leading her to the makeshift dance floor and requesting the DJ to play *"Thinkin' about you,"* by Frank Ocean. Paris laughed and sang along when the first line came booming through the speakers. They wrapped their arms around each other and began to sway to the beat. It was one of their favorite songs because it was the song he played for her when she first rejected him.

"And you thought you'd get rid of me that easily," Maleek chuckled. "You played your cards right."

They didn't realize that a crowd of people had encircled them until they began to chant "Kiss her! Kiss her!" and with Maleek not being one to be told twice, tilted her head towards him with a finger under her chin and kissed her while the crowd cheered.

Chapter 8

"Your phone has been ringing all morning baby, I think you should answer," Maleek told Paris.

"No, no, we promised to spend the day together without our phones. Whoever it is will have to wait till tomorrow."

"What if it's an emergency?"

"Emergency?" she snorted. "Honey, anyone who knows us would have called you or the house phone by now if it was an emergency. I bet it's just a client who wants me to do some last-minute work for them. I've been getting a lot of those lately."

Paris was determined to spend the day with her husband with no distractions. Things had been better than they had ever been and she wanted to keep it that way. Work always put a damper on their plans, so they agreed to spend the day not checking their phones; it was important to be present.

"Paris, just check your phone baby, please? I don't want you to feel guilty later. If it's nothing, you can just ignore it, but at least make sure it's nothing serious." Maleek implored her.

He put her phone next to her and disappeared into the bathroom to take a shower so she could have some privacy. "I'll join you in a minute!" she called out with a smile on her face and unlocked her phone to find 14 missed calls and a text message from Derrick.

Derrick: I need your help.

Her heart raced as she read the message repeatedly. "Is he in trouble? Is he sick?" she whispered to herself. It turns out Maleek was right. She would have been kicking herself had she not checked her phone.

She ran to the walk-in closet and pulled out a pair of blue jeans and a plain black t- shirt. With each passing second, she felt as though she was wasting precious time, so she didn't bother doing her hair and make-up and ran out of the house after telling Maleek she had to go help a friend and would be back soon.

Derrick texted her the address which she immediately recognized as a hotel. It wasn't one of those fancy hotels that everybody knew about, which already caused warning bells to go off in her head. The only reason she knew about this hotel was that she had worked with them before for a client.

All she could think about on the way up to his room was that something bad had happened. Derrick had never asked her for help before, neither did he seem like the type of person to ask for help at all. In the short time, she had known him, she noticed how he loved to care for others. He had even proven it to her when he took care of her when her hand was injured.

Derrick opened the door a few seconds after she knocked and she froze in place. He didn't look sick or troubled. In fact, it didn't seem like anything was wrong at all. He greeted her with a lazy smile wearing nothing but a white towel around his waist.

"What the hell is this?" Paris gritted her teeth in anger.

"I needed to see you." He replied nonchalantly.

Paris scoffed and shook her head. "So you lied to me? I rushed over here thinking something bad had happened and you have the nerve to stand there smiling like you've just won the lottery?"

"I feel like I've won the lottery because you're here and I had bet on you not coming."

"Then why did you call me a million times, Derrick! Why did you text me that you needed help!"

"Calm down, baby.

"Don't you dare call me that!"

"What did you tell your husband?" he smirked.

"You know what? I don't need this. Lose my number." she snarled.

Derrick reached out and grabbed her hand before she had even taken a step and pulled her into the room. She tried to fight him off but her body turned weak the moment their lips collided. All those weeks of trying to forget him were pointless because she couldn't resist his touch. She leaned into him in desperation and he took that as a sign.

The vibrating of her phone interrupted their sexcapade. Paris was so drunk on passion that she didn't realize that two whole hours had gone by. "Oh no!" she cried out and tried to get off Derrick whom she had straddled, but his firm grip kept her in place.

"I have to go. That must be Maleek calling," she panicked.

"I'll let you go once we finish what we started," he moaned and bit into her shoulder a little harder to leave a mark.

"Derrick, stop! Maleek will kill me."

"I can take care of that for you," he chuckled and continued what he was doing.

"What do you mean by that?"

"I'm kidding. Now, stop talking about him and finish what you started."

"This is the third round, Derrick. Please, let me go now."

"Finish what you started," he whispered seductively and trailed his tongue to her nipple.

His distraction worked perfectly because she was back in it. All thoughts of Maleek vanished as she gave in to her innermost desires and let Derrick take her to new heights of pleasure. It was only the second time they were intimate, but Derrick was far better than their first encounter.

After two more rounds of passion, Paris collapsed on the bed next to Derrick and promptly fell asleep. He was insatiable. Each time she wanted to stop he would introduce something new or touch her in a way that awakened all her senses once again. It was an endless cycle of passion that Paris couldn't get used to but enjoyed all the same.

Derrick peppered kisses on her exposed back to wake her up a few hours later. "Wake up sweetheart."

"Five more minutes," she mumbled.

"You've been asleep for five hours Paris," he chuckled in amusement.

Paris' eyes shot open and she scrambled to get out of bed not even caring that she was completely naked. She searched everywhere for her clothes but they were nowhere to be found.

"Give me my clothes, Derrick." She said coldly.

He got up from the bed and strolled to her confidently. "Relax sweetheart, I asked housekeeping to go out and buy the same items. I don't think you remember, but I ripped them off you earlier."

"Even my jeans?"

"Everything down to your panties sugar."

Paris wrapped her arms around herself to cover what she could which made Derrick chuckle. He disappeared into what she presumed was the bathroom, and returned with a white robe.

"Thanks," she said shyly.

"Your clothes won't be here for a while so just relax."

They ended up having dinner in bed while watching a movie.

Just like the last time, Derrick felt comfortable. He was someone she could be around for hours and not get tired of. Everything about him was inviting.

"You're slick," she told him when the movie ended. "I am?"

"Don't act all innocent now," she rolled her eyes. "You knew exactly how to get me here."

"I'd like to believe you came because you wanted to."

"I still have to go back to my husband," she told him straight.

"Why? Clearly you want to be with me. You can deny it all you want but your body can't lie."

Paris shifted uncomfortably to hide her arousal. He was right. Her body wanted him, but her heart wanted Maleek. She would never stop loving Maleek.

"My body might want a hundred other men, but my heart will never waver."

"So you're saying you'd have sex with a hundred men for pleasure as long as you can go home to your husband at the end of the day?"

Paris frowned and replayed the question in her mind but it still made no sense. "That's a twisted question."

"I'm just repeating what you said," he shrugged innocently.

She crossed her arms and eyed him suspiciously. "But that's not what I said. You're twisting my words."

"That's what I heard."

"I already told you, Derrick, I'm not leaving my husband for you." "And I accept that." He nodded calmly.

"Then what do you want from me?"

"Your body and perhaps a little more of your time. I have accepted that I cannot have your heart, but today is proof that I can have your body, and that's what I want."

"I'm going home."

"You'll be back."

Paris took her car keys and phone off and walked out in her robe. The longer she stayed with Derrick the more confused she felt about what she wanted. What scared her the most was that he was right; she rushed over to him because her body was drawn to him. The attraction they shared was electric; unlike anything, she had ever felt before.

Walking into *Nordstrom* wearing nothing but a robe was the most embarrassing moment of Paris' life. She would have gone to

Walmart but Maleek would notice the second she walked in that those were not her clothes. He knew what all her clothing looked like, so if she had to replace anything she'd go back to the exact stores she originally purchased them from.

The drive back home was more nerve-wracking than walking into a store in a robe. She couldn't think of any excuse that Maleek would find acceptable so she decided to call Monique for help.

"Hey sis!" Monique answered on the fifth ring.

"Hey Mo, listen, I need you to cover for me with Maleek." "Ooh, has someone been naughty?" Monique giggled.

"I had to go help a friend that Maleek would not approve of," Paris lied. "Can you please tell him I was helping you?"

"Okay, but who is this friend that I've never heard of? I know all your friends, and Maleek doesn't have an issue with any of them."

"I'll explain everything another time, just please do this for me?"

"I've got your back Jack!"

"Thank you. I'll talk to you later."

Paris thought she would have to launch into an explanation the minute she stepped into the house but Maleek shocked her by greeting her with a smile and a sweet kiss.

"What was that for?" she frowned in confusion.

"Monique just called to check if you arrived safely. She told me what you did for her today."

"She did?"

"Yes, and I made dinner for the best wife on the planet."

Paris didn't know what lie Monique had cooked up, but she was grateful that she didn't have to lie to Maleek's face. If anything, she hoped to preserve the faith and trust that he had in her.

Chapter 9

"I feel like a new man!" Maleek exclaimed. He was telling Paris all about his therapy and the stories he's heard that were similar to his. Paris feigned interest but in reality, she was anxious to hear from Derrick. He had gone off the radar again.

It bothered her how easily he could disappear and reappear whenever he wanted to. It was unnerving to know that he knew where to find her but she had no idea where to begin when it came to finding him.

"… Can you believe that? Honestly, I always looked down on therapy because, you know, black folk don't believe in it, but group therapy has been a game changer, don't you agree?"

Paris kept nodding long after Maleek had stopped talking and he noticed. Even a bat could see that although she was physically there, she was not present.

"Paris? Did you hear what I said?"

"Of course, honey. You said you love therapy."

Maleek sighed and knelt in front of his wife. "What's going on Paris? You've been anxious and distracted all week. The only time you look remotely excited is when you get a text messages. Talk to me."

"I'm alright my love," she faked a smile.

"Don't lie to me, Paris. I know something is going on. Even the kids have noticed." "Okay, fine," she sighed dramatically.

"I've been planning a surprise party for you, now you've ruined it."

"A surprise party? Honey, my birthday is 5 months away," he chuckled. "I knew you were obsessed with being organized, but this is a new record."

"Yeah, well I had a big vision for it so I had to start planning early. Do you know how hard it is to book a good venue? You have to do it months in advance!"

"Okay, okay, I'm sorry for ruining the surprise. I've just been wondering where you've been disappearing to."

"Well, now that you know you better keep your nose out of it and you better act surprised on the day."

"Yes ma'am!" he saluted her and left for work.

Guilt- something she had become used to- washed over her immediately. She had never been a good liar, and now she was unashamedly lying to her husband. "Great, now I have to plan a party," she groaned.

Because Maleek had agreed to drop the kids off that morning, Paris had time to come up with a game plan. Derrick was not taking her calls or replying to her texts, so she was going to smoke him out of wherever he was hiding.

"He can't disappear, he's a cop," she mused. "He's a cop!"

Paris remembered the words written on the police vehicle he was driving when he escorted her home and knew exactly where to start. After scarfing down her breakfast, she ran upstairs to pick out the perfect outfit.

She felt possessed. Logic said she should thank her lucky stars and be grateful that he had finally left her alone, but the problem was she was the one who wanted him now. "So this is how he felt when I ignored him," she pouted.

The outfit Paris picked out was what the kids would refer to as a "thirst trap". She had never been one to expose her body, but Derrick brought that side out of her. He made her feel desirable and sexy, and that was what she wanted to portray.

What she laid out on her bed was a black bodycon mini dress that hugged her hourglass figure like a glove and black open toed thigh-high boots. Because she wanted to maintain a level of dignity, she threw a long beige coat over it, but knowing Derrick, her dignity would be out the window faster than she could take her clothes off.

Driving to the police station turned her on. Just the thought of being around all those officers in her sexy outfit was enough to get her going. There was just something about a man in that navy blue uniform with a gun on his hip that was a complete turn on to her. She was so excited to see the look on Derrick's face when she walked in.

Strangely, she didn't know what position he held or if he was transferred to another district. She could only hope that her plan would be executed exactly how she envisioned it. Paris sauntered into the police station with her head held high and asked to see Derrick.

Everyone looked at her like she had grown a second head so she repeated herself. "I'm here to see Derrick Brown."

"Ma'am, you can't just stroll in and demand to see Captain Brown without an appointment."

"Captain? He's a captain?"

"Seeing as you are unaware of this fact, I am inclined to believe that you are one of the women who have been stalking the captain and I'm going to have to ask you to leave, ma'am."

"No, no, I know Derrick. We just don't talk about work and stuff."

"I will not repeat myself, ma'am."

"That's okay officer Stanley," Derrick's smooth voice interrupted their standoff. "She's good. Let her in."

"My apologies ma'am," Officer Stanley said and stepped aside.

Paris smiled and walked past him with the same confidence she had when she strode in. She was surprised by how huge the station was. Truthfully, she had never been to this side of town, let alone visited a police station, so it was interesting to see.

"So you're a captain huh?" she playfully nudged Derrick. They were walking side by side to his office, careful not to raise any suspicion.

"Yes ma'am, I am."

"I have so many questions," she said when they got to his office and he shut the door. "But first…"

Paris spun around and dropped her coat to reveal her freakum dress. She rejoiced internally when Derrick's eyes traveled the length of her body. This was exactly what she wanted. He called the shots the last time they met, but this time she was in charge.

"Sit down captain," she commanded him and he obliged.

After doing unspeakable things to him in a station full of officers, Paris promised him she would be back for more and left with a satisfied smirk on her face. Now that she knew where to find him, she was going to take advantage of this new information as often as possible.

Instead of going home, she remained in the parking lot until Derrick came out and then she tailed him. It had only been a few hours but she was aching for him again, so she followed at a safe distance until he got to a residential area that she recognized. He obviously hadn't spotted her yet because she and Maleek had switched cars for the day.

She approached a red light and ran her fingers through her hair when "What are you doing Paris? This is crazy."

That speech she had given Derrick about being nothing more

than friends had come back to bite her because she was the one craving his presence now. He was all she could think about. Not even Sex with Maleek could help her get over Derrick. Everything Maleek did in the bedroom paled in comparison to Derrick's skills.

A knock on her window startled her. Everyone and everything seemed to be startling her these days. She lowered her window so she could hear what Derrick was saying. She didn't care that he'd caught her, she just wanted his attention.

"You're asking for trouble sugar," he warned.

"Will I be punished Mr. Officer?" she asked seductively.

Instead of responding, Derrick walked around the car and sat in the passenger seat. "Drive," he commanded.

"Where are we going?" "Just drive."

The intoxicating scent of his cologne filled the car and had her biting her lip in arousal. But he sat ever so calmly and unbothered as though her presence did nothing for him, and it upset her.

"You're upset," he said as though stating a fact.

"Damn right I'm upset," she shot back. "I'm barely keeping it together and you're here unbothered."

Derrick took her free hand and guided it down to his crotch

where she felt his hardness. He wasn't silent because he was unbothered, rather, he was silent because he was practicing self-control.

"Keep your eyes on the road," he instructed her, but she couldn't take it anymore.

Paris had come to terms with the fact that she was addicted to Derrick, and she wasn't going to fight it anymore. Her 'situationship' with Derrick made her understand why Maleek couldn't stop. It was addictive.

She pulled into an alley between a grocery store and a bakery and dropped her seat all the way down before climbing over and straddling Derrick. "I can't wait any longer," she told him between desperate kisses.

"You're addicted to me, sugar," he growled and buried his face between her breasts. "What will you do about it?" she challenged him.

They rocked the car back and forth until someone banged on the window and yelled at them to find a hotel or they'd call the cops. Paris and Derrick burst into laughter and finished off before driving to a more secluded location to continue their sex frenzy.

Before she dropped him off, Paris took a few photos and videos of them in the act and sent them to Derrick's phone. She pulled him in for a deep kiss and instructed him to pleasure himself to the photos and videos later, promising to do the same after her husband fell asleep.

"Lose the thong next time," he retorted. "Otherwise, I'll have to keep replacing them and I've got better things to do with my money."

He kissed her one more time and she drove off into the night fully satiated as expected. Derrick was a phenomenal lover. "Damn it! I have to plan a party!" she groaned.

Chapter 10

"So, now that we have all that 'how have you been' nonsense out of the way, tell me, where have you been and what's keeping you so busy these days?"

"Planning a surprise party," Paris replied seamlessly. "It's far more stressful than I imagined. Plus I have a new client who insists on having meetings multiple times a week."

Monique burst out laughing. "I thought the surprise party was just a cover-up story." "It's real, my friend. I had to hire a professional party planner to help me," Paris sighed dramatically.

"That's good then. I was almost offended thinking you were keeping secrets from me."

"Never! I barely have time between the planning and the new client. I swear I'll need a vacation when this is all over."

"I bet Maleek would love that. The two of you look so much happier lately. What's your secret?"

"We've been working on our communication and reconnecting in other ways if you know what I mean," Paris wiggled her eyebrows.

"No wonder Maleek hasn't been sleeping around lately."

Paris frowned and raised her eyebrow at her friend. "How do you know that he hasn't been messing around lately?"

"Come on, Paris. I've got eyes and ears everywhere. Plus, I threatened to torture him if he didn't get his act together."

"You're crazy!" Paris laughed. "But thanks for being such a great friend. It feels good to know that someone has my back."

"Always."

"Mo, I've got a meeting with a new client so I have to get out of here. I can't be late. Love ya!"

Paris had been getting so many new clients that she was thinking of just setting up an office where she could work full-time. It had never crossed her mind until the sudden influx of clients.

Her latest client, Melody Brown, was starting a business and was interested in a long- term contract, which was exciting. They agreed to meet at the new restaurant that had just opened downtown. They had only spoken via email, but Paris felt connected to her. She had a feeling that she would love working with this woman and that they would build a good relationship.

Paris arrived first and set up her laptop. After half an hour of waiting, a gorgeous African American woman walked in. She was the epitome of class. Her hair was neatly styled in a bun, and her dress screamed old Hollywood glam. She was a sight to behold.

"So, you're Paris Johnson," Ms. Brown said coldly.

"Yes I am," Paris replied cheerfully. "It's a pleasure to meet you Ms. Brown." "Tell me more about yourself, Paris."

"Well, I have two degrees; one in-"

"I don't care about that," Ms. Brown cut her off. "Tell me about yourself. Are you married? Do you have kids? That sort of thing."

"Oh, okay. Um, I prefer to keep things professional though."

"And I prefer to get personal with people I'll be working with."

Paris took a swig of water and relaxed in her seat. "Fair enough. Well, I am in fact married. I have two kids, and I work from home. How about you?"

Ms. Brown smiled bitterly while drawing imaginary lines on the table. "I'm married. We don't have kids because I can't bear children. Actually, I think you might *know* my husband."

"I don't think so. I don't have any male friends."

Melody looked Paris dead in the eyes without blinking. "The pictures on Derrick Brown's phone state otherwise."

Paris inhaled sharply and reached for her glass of water, which was unfortunately empty. The exit seemed so far away, but even then, she still had to pack up her computer, so she couldn't make a quick escape.

"I was wondering who had my husband's attention," Melody continued. "He comes home late; doesn't eat my cooking; doesn't have sex with me. I can see why though. Derrick has always been attracted to *thick* women. I was the exception."

"I don't need you to say anything, Paris. I don't think you can anyway. All I ask is that you stay away from my husband. I'm not interested in cat fights, all I need is my husband back. You're a woman so I'm sure you know how painful it is to be cheated on. I don't want to break up your family, so please don't break up mine."

Melody Brown got up and walked out as classy as she did when she arrived. Paris looked around to see if anyone had listened in on their conversation, but the tables around her were empty. She breathed a sigh of relief and took out her phone to text Derrick.

Paris: We need to talk ASAP.

Derrick: Meet me at the same hotel and room as last time at 6 pm.

There was too much time to kill but Paris' anxiety was through the roof, so she decided to go to the hotel early to take a nap. All the sneaking around had her constantly on edge so she was in desperate need of a reset. It baffled her when she realized the level of stress her husband had gone through trying to hide his infidelities; it felt like a full-time job.

Derrick walked in on time, as usual, and peppered Paris with light kisses. "Wake up, sleeping beauty."

Paris sat up, putting a bit of distance between her and Derrick, which of course, did not go unnoticed by him; he had a very sharp eye. As expected, he frowned and tried to close the gap between them, but she moved further away.

"You didn't tell me you were married," she sulked.

Derrick exhaled and pinched the bridge of his nose. This meant he was frustrated, as Paris had come to know. At least he wasn't rubbing his chin, which meant he was angry. His eyes became cold and distant which infuriated Paris. Even though she was married, she had been honest about her situation from the get-go.

"Aren't you going to explain?"

"Why should I explain myself to you? Aren't you married too?" he growled.

She stood up and matched his energy. "The difference is I have been honest with you this whole time, and my husband hasn't hunted you down yet."

"What difference does it make? You're addicted to me," he smirked. "You couldn't stay away from me even if I had six wives. Face it, you're mine."

"Fuck you!" she retaliated. "I can deal with many things, but I hate liars. Stay the hell away from me."

With that she stormed out, slamming the door behind her. It felt empowering to end things on her terms. Well, it had always been on her terms so technically she was selfishly calling the shots. Guilt- her new friend- couldn't take over this time because Derrick had lied to her when she had trusted him completely.

It was embarrassing enough to meet his wife. That encounter made her feel small and dirty, and she never wanted to feel that way again, so she convinced herself that she was done with him.

A few days later, Paris was hit with an intense desire that she could not control. She had been ignoring Derrick's texts and calls so he was not an option. Instead, she grabbed her husband at every option and ravaged him like a crazy woman.

"Whoa! Hold up," Maleek held her at arms-length when she ambushed him in the laundry room.

"I need you right now baby. Please." She begged while simultaneously trying to undress him.

"Paris, stop." He said firmly. "I love you, and I love making love to you, but this is too much."

"It was never too much with your hoes!" she yelled and burst into tears.

Maleek was clearly hurt, but he still embraced her until she calmed down. "You promised not to throw that in my face when you get upset," he sighed.

"I'm sorry," she mumbled into his chest.

"We have to take it easy, my love. I'm trying to get over an addiction I've had for over a decade. The more I engage in sex the more I desire it and can't control myself. I know it's hard but just give me some time, please. We can still do it 3 times a week as we've always done, but not more than that for now, okay?"

Paris nodded and walked out with her head hung low. Her body was aching for release, but she couldn't go back to Derrick; she had more self-respect than that. After doing some research, she purchased some toys so she could get it done herself, but they weren't as good as the real thing.

Each day that went by was more unbearable than the last. It felt like an itch that she could not scratch. Everything she tried didn't satisfy her, not even the few times she and Maleek made love. All roads were leading back to Derrick, but she kept fighting it.

Maleek was going away on a business trip for a day, so she asked Monique to watch the kids and drove to the hotel where Derrick was waiting for her. They both knew it was on when she finally answered his call. Derrick had a smug smile on his face when he opened the door.

"Shut up," she grumbled and pushed past him into the room.

Chapter 11

"What do you think about running away and starting a new life together?" Derrick suggested.

"You know the answer to that already."

They were lying in bed entangled in one another talking about their lives. She learned that Derrick was an only child, married his wife to please his family, and it was his dream to become a captain. These were things he had never revealed before, and had she not forced him, he probably wouldn't have spoken about them ever.

"But seriously, Paris. You and I make sense. No one else can satisfy me like you do, and I know I do the same for you."

"I can't argue with that, but the thing is, I love my husband and my kids, you know that."

"Then why are you in bed with me right now?" he challenged. "Do you want me to leave? Because you know I will."

Derrick shut her up with a kiss, making sure she stayed in place. The lines had become blurred, so she had to keep reminding herself that she loved Maleek. Her affair had become more than just a physical act. She found herself thinking about Derrick throughout the day and wondering what he was doing and where he was. There was an undeniable emotional connection between them that kept her coming back for more.

"How's the planning going?" Monique asked her when she got back home. "I think it's going to be the party of the year," Paris exclaimed. What everyone didn't know was that she had left everything in the hands of the planner. All the days they were meant to have meetings she spent in Derrick's arms. She was confident in her deception because she had all the bases covered; nothing could go wrong at this point.

"I bet Maleek will love it," Monique sighed dreamily. "Let me know if you need help."

"I will. By the way, how is it going in the relationship department?"

Monique became giddy instantly but she made sure the kids were out of earshot first before she said, "I'm in love!"

Paris choked on her water and stared at her best friend in shock. "How come this is the first I'm hearing of this? I need all the details right now. Come on, spill the tea!"

"His name is Joshua."

Paris squealed and hugged her best friend. "That's Maleek's middle name! You and I were meant to be."

"That isn't even the crazy part," Monique giggled. "He's also an engineer!"

"Girl! We can be neighbors now!" Paris squealed. "My neighbor is selling his house, so you and Joshua can move in."

"Slow down!" Monique laughed. "We're taking things slow."

"Tell me more then! Does he have kids? What's his credit score? Is he short or tall?

Does he have a crazy momma? Tell me everything."

"I will… next time." Monique grinned mischievously. "I hate you," Paris sulked.

"I have to go. I'm surprising him with lunch."

Paris walked Monique to the door and they were both startled by the woman standing on the other side of the door. Paris gulped, knowing who she was, but Monique smiled and greeted her enthusiastically after noticing her designer bag.

"Mo, you have to go, remember? You don't want to be late to your appointment," Paris nudged her friend.

"Right! I almost forgot about that. Bye babe!"

Melody Brown didn't take her eyes off Paris for a second. She seemed angry, judging by her clenched jaw. This time she was dressed in black palazzo pants and a fitted white blouse. It wasn't an outfit to fight in, but her energy felt vicious.

Melody took a step forward with her top lip curled in disgust. "I was hoping it wouldn't come to this, but I see you didn't take me seriously the first time."

"Now you're stalking me?" Paris asked with a straight face.

"Mrs. Johnson, does your husband know that he shares you with another man?" "Shouldn't you be asking your husband why he's not satisfied with you?" Paris fired back.

Melody flinched ever so slightly. If Paris hadn't been paying attention she would have missed the minute movement. She celebrated internally thinking she had rattled Melody when it shouldn't have been a competition, to begin with. Derrick was married to Melody, so the right thing to do was to stop seeing him, but Paris had never been one to back down from a fight.

"I think I've been very kind and understanding thus far," Melody said with a sweet smile on her face. "I have to say, Mrs. Johnson, my patience is wearing thin. This serves as a final warning; stay away from my husband, or I'll have to tell your husband and dear children what's been keeping you busy lately."

"You'd really risk ruining your husband's reputation just to get back at me? Well, since that's how you want to play it, let's do it."

Melody fully grinned for the first time since they met and it was the scariest thing Paris had ever seen. She was undoubtedly beautiful, but her smile looked downright evil.

"Oh, I forgot to tell you that I am an attorney, so I know how to clean up Derrick's messes. What will you do about your situation? I doubt graphic design can help you fix your family."

"I'm not afraid of you, Melody. Do your worst. Maleek will never leave me."

"Oh yeah? Shall we find out? Mm, I'm going to enjoy this more than I thought. See you later then, Paris."

Melody swayed her hips as she walked way. It would have been comical had she not just threatened to turn Paris's life upside down. There was something about the way she talked that sent chills down Paris's spine. Melody seemed like a very dangerous woman, but Paris was from the streets. Losing was not a part of her vocabulary.

Paris was on edge for the rest of the day. Her eyes were peeled on the driveway each time a car drove by. Now that Melody knew where they lived she could show up at any time and ruin their lives. Staying in the house made Paris feel like a sitting duck so she called a sitter so she could go out for dinner with her husband. A change in scenery was what she needed to organize her thoughts.

Maleek tried to get out of going because he was exhausted, but she begged him until he gave in. There was a nice Italian restaurant that she had been dying to visit and this was her chance, plus she loved dressing up whenever she got the chance.

"Is that what you're wearing?" Maleek frowned when she walked downstairs in a figure-hugging red dress with a slit that was a little too high for Maleek's liking.

"I'll never have another opportunity to wear this, so let me be."

"Every man will be staring at you," he complained.

"True. But you'll be the one I'm going home with and if you play your cards right you'll be the one that gets to take this little number off me."

That logic was enough to convince Maleek. She knew how to play to his ego; it always worked. He was humble in many areas, but he was still a man. And he loved to show her off to his friends, colleagues, and any other man that he caught admiring her beauty.

The restaurant turned out to be even better than Paris had imagined. Since it had just opened, they were greeted by the owner, who offered them the best table in the house because of how well they were dressed. Thankfully it wasn't packed so they could enjoy a quiet romantic dinner together.

They were reminiscing about their wedding day when Paris looked up and stiffened. Coming straight to their table was Derrick and Melody. They looked like the perfect couple walking hand in hand and smiling lovingly.

"What a coincidence!" Melody chirped happily. "May we join you? Make it a double date?"

Maleek looked at her and back at Paris and replied with a suspicious tone almost as if he had seen a ghost or as if he were already familiar with at least one piece of the couple. "I'm sorry, who are you?"

"We're Paris's friends," Melody answered without hesitation.

"I'm surprised she's never mentioned us to you before."

"Oh! I think I know who you are," Maleek forced a half smile and lightly nudged his wife. "This one has been planning a 'surprise' party for me. You must be the party planner."

Melody looked elated and played along. Maleek had unknowingly given her more ammunition to use against Paris. "Smart man!"

"Please, join us," Maleek offered even after Paris kicked him under the table and lightly shook her head.

Maleek and Melody instantly hit it off. Almost as if they already knew each other. They didn't even notice that Derrick and Paris had been silent the whole time. The only words Derrick had spoken the whole night was when he introduced himself to Maleek.

Paris kept her eyes on her food the whole time to avoid Derrick's piercing gaze. She couldn't believe that he was openly ogling her. He was behaving as though Maleek wasn't even there. What's worse is that Melody kept distracting Maleek each time he glanced at Derrick. It was as if she was helping Derrick get away with his behavior, which was weird because she had threatened Paris earlier that day.

"We should do this again soon," Maleek suggested. "We would love that," Melody replied.

Maleek, Derrick, and Melody, all had different expressions on their faces when Paris excused herself and stood up. Maleek looked at her lovingly, Derrick looked at her lustfully, and Melody looked like she was ready to kill her. Paris instantly regretted her outfit choice, but she still strutted away confidently.

She didn't know what would be said while she was away. All she could do was pray that Melody didn't rat her out. Admittedly, she hadn't taken Melody's threat seriously until they showed up in the restaurant. It was apparent that she was being watched and maybe even followed.

"Oh God," Paris exhaled when she got to the restroom. "What do I do now?"

Chapter 12

Paris finally decided to stay away from Derrick for good, and this time she meant it. He and his wife were obviously bad news. It was evident that they were playing a sick game and she was a pawn in it. Every time she remembered the looks on their faces when they strolled into the restaurant a few weeks ago made her want to throw up.

This time she was serious and Derrick finally learned how serious she was. Merely blocking his number wasn't enough because he would call from different numbers until he heard her voice, so she changed her number altogether.

She thought she would have peace once the phone calls stopped, but Derrick began to leave random gifts and notes either on the doorstep or on the hood of her car. This didn't only happen when she was at home. She would find random objects and notes on her car even when she went to the grocery store or Monique's house. It was like Derrick was everywhere.

Paris was constantly on edge because of this. It got so bad that she had to get medication from the doctor for her anxiety and insomnia. She had no way out of this hell. There was no one to talk to who could possibly understand the situation and help her. Derrick was a police captain, so he had a level of power and influence that she couldn't compete with.

After weeks of mental torture, Paris couldn't handle it anymore. All the TV shows she watched ended in the stalker or the victim dying, so she decided to end her life before he got the chance to. She had changed her number three times already, and each time he somehow got it and continued his harassment.

She no longer felt safe in her own home, or even going anywhere alone. Her paranoia caused her to begin to hallucinate. She kept seeing Derrick standing at street corners watching her or following her home in different vehicles every day. The situation had escalated faster than she could wrap her head around what was happening.

Melody had suddenly disappeared. Her threats ended up being just that; she never followed through. But Derrick, the seemingly sweet officer, had become a thorn in her flesh. But she refused to let him win.

"I'd rather die than let him have me," she'd mumble to herself every morning.

She had her suicide planned perfectly. First, she was going to cook a big breakfast for her family, tell them she loves them, and then she would kiss Maleek goodbye, and drive the kids to school. The final step to her plan was to swallow a handful of pills and drive off a bridge. She didn't want any hope of survival.

One would think her decision was based solely on the stalking, when in fact the guilt of what she had done was slowly eating her up. Maleek promised to change, and indeed he had. Even their family and friends could tell that he was a changed man. No one took it seriously at first, but it was undeniable now that months had gone by. He had become so transparent that she couldn't doubt him even if she wanted to.

The breakfast went as planned. Maleek and the kids were delighted to eat all their favorite foods that they didn't notice her somber mood. They didn't know that this would be the last time they would see her alive.

The kids rambled about things she didn't understand on the way to their school. Every sentence had the word "lit" in it. She watched them through the rearview mirror and smiled. This would be the last time she'd get to see those faces.

"Have a good day, and don't ever forget that I love you," she told them when they arrived in front of the school.

"I love you too mom, but don't say that in front of my friends; it'll ruin my street cred." Junior replied.

Paris chuckled and told them to hurry so they wouldn't be late. "What street cred?" she chuckled as she drove off.

The screen in the car signaled that Monique was calling. It was odd because she was supposed to be at work, and she never called from work. "Hey baby," Paris teased. It always got on Monique's nerves because it "reminded her of her singleness".

"Hey Sugar, did you miss me," Derrick chuckled.

Paris swerved the car in fear, almost causing an accident. She rubbed her eyes and checked the screen again. Indeed it was Monique's name that was written on it. Her mind instantly conjured up every terrible scenario of what could have happened to Monique.

"Where's Monique? What have you done to her you bastard!"

"Shhh, don't get all worked up. I don't want you to have to be put on anymore medication."

"H-how did you know about that," Paris shuddered.

"I'm all knowing, Sugar," he replied calmly. "I just called to warn you not to do anything stupid unless you want your precious friend to suffer the consequences meant for your stupid ass. Or better yet, your kids look strong enough to endure a little torture."

"No, no, no, Derrick, please don't hurt my kids," she sobbed.

"Oh come now, I'm not a monster. I won't lay a finger on them, but I know a few people who aren't as kind as I am."

"Fine, I'll play along. Just leave them out of this… I beg you."

"Mm, I love it when you beg," he moaned. "Okay, since I'm so generous, I'll guarantee you their safety, but I want you."

"Please, no. Anything but that," she cried out.

"I thought you might say that. Well, I could just show your husband all the footage from the hotel."

Paris sobbed in agony when he said that. She should have known that something like this would happen. She should have known she was being recorded because they never changed rooms… she should have known better.

"Okay, okay, I'll meet you at the hotel," she conceded.

"Hotel?" he scoffed. "Sugar, you've been a bad girl. Hotels are for good girls. Oh no, no, no, you deserve to be punished for your disobedience."

"Derrick, please…"

"You deserve to be bent over in front of a dumpster in a dark alley and treated like the worthless bitch that you are. I'll text you the address. You better show up in 10 minutes or else."

The humiliation and degradation alone were enough to wish for death. As Derrick rammed into her over and over while she was bent over a pile of trash, she silently cried and wished she had never fantasized about this. Thinking it would feel good to be raped by an officer was the worst thing she had ever hoped for. This wasn't the passionate love-making she had been accustomed to with Derrick. It was dirty, painful, and demeaning.

Derrick yanked her head back by her hair and growled in her ear. "You better show up when I call you Bitch! No excuses." He threw her on the ground and instructed her to clean herself up and get dressed.

"Is Monique okay?" she sniffled.

"Who?" he chuckled. "Ah! Your friend. I'm sure she's okay. She was incredibly happy when I returned her phone. That foolish girl even asked me out on a date."

"You lied to me?" she said incredulously.

He smirked and walked away, leaving her alone in the alley. She pulled her pants up and ran back to her car. She figured she still had time to kill herself. Derrick had proved that he was bluffing the first time, so she was set on carrying out her plan. But her gut told her he was far more dangerous than she thought, so she turned her car around and headed back home to scrub off the filth of his touch.

"I'm not weak," she sobbed as she scrubbed her body raw. "You don't own me, you sick bastard."

She felt decent again after about an hour in the shower. The time alone and the heat of the water helped her think straight. Being a victim would never be a part of her vocabulary ever again. Instead of weeping and trembling in front of Derrick, she was going to beat him at his own game.

But first, she needed to tell someone what was happening. The biggest mistake she had made since beginning this affair was keeping it a secret. Yes, what she had done was wrong, but she should have trusted her instinct when she first saw the red flags.

She texted him to let him know that she would do whatever he asked as long as he kept his wife in check, just to assert some dominance. If she played her cards right, she would come out on top, but in order to do that she had to get at least one person on her side; someone who wouldn't judge her for the mistakes she made, and that could only be Monique.

"I hope I'm not making a mistake," she mused. "I can't afford to make a mistake."

Chapter 13

Monique listened intently the whole time Paris was explaining her situation. For as long as they had known each other, Paris had been the tamer of the two so it was shocking to hear her talk about her crazy fantasies and all the nasty things she did with the officer.

"Say something," Paris whimpered.

Monique shifted uncomfortably in her seat trying to choose her words carefully. "Honestly, I'm shocked but a little proud. I didn't think you had it in you."

"What should I do!"

Monique rolled her eyes dramatically. "You have to keep seeing him of course."

"Are you insane? Why would I do that?"

"Paris, this man is clearly obsessed with you and he is in a position to make your life a living hell. I know it's not what you want to hear, but until we find something we can use against him, you're going to have to play along."

"Can't I just run away? Or kill myself."

Monique stood up and slapped Paris unexpectedly. "Don't you dare do anything stupid."

Paris dropped her head to hide the tears that rolled down her face. "It's all too much. I'm not mentally equipped for this."

"You have no choice babe. I know men like him. This will only end on his terms unless you have the upper hand."

"But what happens after Maleek's party? He'll definitely know something's up if I keep disappearing for long hours."

"Don't worry about him, I'll take of Maleek and cover for you. I'll cause as many distractions as I need to so he doesn't find out. I promise you that."

"What would I do without you, Mo," Paris cried.

And just as she said, Monique covered for Paris whenever Maleek got suspicious. She did so all while staying hard at work trying to dig up dirt on Derrick. His squeaky clean image was too good to be true, as she had found out the hard way, but she knew there had to be a crack somewhere.

Monique advised her to revert to how she acted in the beginning and seek out Derrick instead of waiting on him to order her around. This way she had a bit of power and was not subjected to humiliating situations. So Paris began to plan "spontaneous" encounters with Derrick, which he loved.

He praised her on her obedience and promised to treat her well if she stayed in line. As disgusted as she was, Paris agreed with a sweet smile on her face. Monique had warned her not to give Derrick any reason to be suspicious.

"Don't even change your speech pattern," Monique instructed her. "He'll quickly figure you out if you do too much. Consistency is the key."

"So I shouldn't tell him I love him or that I'll leave Maleek for him?"

"Bingo! You've been adamant on staying with Maleek for months. It'll be odd to suddenly change your mind. Just don't do anything too drastic or out of character." Monique emphasized.

"Okay, and what do we do about his wife?" "We kill her," Monique shrugged.

"Please tell me you're joking," Paris replied wide-eyed.

"Of course! Relax, Paris. We're not killing anyone."

Monique came up with the brilliant idea of recording Melody Brown the next time she showed up to threaten Paris. The only catch was that they had to provoke her first, and then make sure she showed up at the right location where the camera would be set up.

All the plotting and scheming was exciting because it would buy Paris her freedom, but it also had her question who exactly her best friend was. Monique had never shown this crafty side in all the years they had known each other. This alone was enough for Paris to tread carefully with the information she shared with Monique.

"Your greatest enemies in life are often those right beside you," Paris's mother would always say while she was growing up.

The plan had been in motion for weeks already, and still, no one suspected a thing.

Paris kept playing her cards right and Derrick began to trust her. She fooled him into agreeing to get rid of his wife because she had failed to lure Melody into her trap; a trap which Derrick was incognizant of.

"Will you finally leave that idiot if I get rid of her?" Derrick asked her one day.

Paris wrapped her arms around his neck and pulled him in for a kiss. "Derrick, I can't do that to my kids."

"We can have kids of our own," he countered.

She mustered up as much self-control as she could to prevent herself from scowling. Derrick was a fool if he ever believed that she'd do anything to hurt her kids. Nevertheless, she had to play along and keep her honest thoughts to herself.

"Why haven't you and Melody had kids yet?" she suddenly asked, hoping to learn some new information about his marriage.

"She doesn't want to mess up her figure," he smiled pensively. "Actually, I think it has more to do with our busy lives. We're both at the peak of our careers."

"Well, I think you would have made a great dad."

Derrick paused for a second and then said, "What made you change your mind about us?"

Paris blinked rapidly but maintained a smile. "Huh? What do you mean?"

"Come to think of it, you wanted nothing to do with me until I borrowed your friend's phone and asked you to meet me," he said innocently.

Paris almost scoffed at this. She couldn't believe how he had twisted the events.

Stealing a phone and threatening her was what he had actually done, not the sugary version he had just given.

"Maleek is cheating again," she lied. "I guess I just got fed up with his lies and decided to live my life the way I wanted to since he's doing the same with his life."

"You see? I told you he didn't deserve you," Derrick nodded thoughtfully.

Being in his arms made her sick, but she promised to bear it until Monique could dig up some dirt on him. There was nothing she would have loved more than kicking Derrick in the nuts and walking out of the room like a hero, but she had to be patient.

Monique called Paris the next day with some good news but said they couldn't talk over the phone and the only time they could meet was in the evening because of work. Paris was on edge the whole day. All she could focus on was the antique clock on her wall ticking away. There was no way she'd be able to get any work done with her curiosity piqued, so she sat on the couch and watched reality TV shows to kill time.

When dinner time rolled around, Paris scarfed down her food like her life depended on it and excused herself. She hated driving at night, but nothing was going to stop her from finding a way to escape the web of lies she had entangled herself.

Monique was high on excitement when Paris walked through the door. They didn't even bother with pleasantries and got right down to business. After all, they had known each other long enough that the small talk was never necessary.

"I found proof that he got promoted through his wife's connections," Monique explained. "There were some shady deals that took place."

"How on earth did you find all of this, Mo? This is top level information!"

"I have my sources," Monique boasted.

"So how do we use this against him?" Paris asked. She didn't want to question Monique further about these mysterious sources because she didn't want to know. Anyone who could get this level of information, along with proof, was a dangerous person.

"That's where I got stuck. See, Derrick is far more intelligent than we thought. On top of that, he has access to the police force and all its systems. Not to mention his wife who can get him out of any legal situation because she's got connections in high places."

"In other words, blackmail is not an option," Paris sighed in defeat.

"Well, at least we now know how dangerous these two are."

"We've known that for weeks, girl. What we need now is a plan. I can't deal with being his slave for life."

Monique jumped out of her seat looking excited and yelling, "I got it!" while she danced around her living room. "Okay, hear me out. Since we can't beat them legally, we can beat them mentally by shifting the target."

Paris furrowed her eyebrows and sat up straight. "What do you mean by that? I don't get it."

"Alright check this: Derrick is obsessed with you, right? So instead of trying to get him in trouble, why don't we find someone he can shift his attention to?"

"I'd hate myself if I let another woman get trapped in this situation. I can't do that."

"Yes you can, Paris! Look, we can find someone who is desperate for money and isn't tied to a husband or kids; someone who wouldn't mind being a mistress. It's perfect, trust me."

Paris sunk back in her seat suddenly feeling exhausted. "And if that doesn't work?" she asked her best friend.

"Then we keep trying until we find a way out," Monique assured her.

Chapter 14

Buridan's donkey is a paradox in which an equally hungry and thirsty donkey is placed midway between a pail of water and a stack of hay. The assumption is that the donkey would die of both hunger and thirst due to indecision because there is no rational choice between the two. Paris was the donkey in a seemingly impossible situation.

The worst had happened; she had fallen for Derrick. When he wasn't threatening her life he pampered her like a queen, not to mention the mind-blowing sex. On the other hand, she had Maleek and her children. Regardless of the choice she made, someone would be devastated in the end.

Amidst her scheming with Monique, it occurred to her that she had developed genuine feelings for Derrick. What complicated the situation was that he was ready to leave his wife for her. Well, so she thought.

"This is Sonya. She has agreed to be Derrick's distraction," Monique said proudly.

Paris frowned and looked Sonya up and down. The young lady was gorgeous without a doubt. She had a tiny waist and a big booty, which was every man's fantasy. The only thing fake about her was her perfectly round and perky breasts.

"Hi," Paris greeted her coldly. The longer she looked at Sonya the more irritated she became. There was something off about the young woman, but Paris had no idea what it was. She seemed too perfect for the job.

"Why did you choose her?" Paris asked Monique. "And where did you find her?"

Monique instructed Sonya to take a seat in the lounge so she could have some privacy with Paris. "What the hell are you doing? I found the perfect candidate and you're trying to sabotage it!"

Paris crossed her arms stubbornly. "I don't like her."

"No one cares! What matters is that Derrick likes her and falls for her."

"She looks like a hooker, Monique. Derrick is a little more classy than that."

"Then we'll give her a makeover," Monique shrugged.

"I'm sure Derrick can sniff out a thot from a mile away."

"Oh, I see what's happening here," Monique laughed. "You have feelings for him, don't you?"

"You know I love Maleek."

"That wasn't the question, Paris. Look you need to figure out what you want and make a choice before Maleek finds out and makes the choice for you."

Although she sulked the whole time, Paris agreed to go with Monique's suggestion. The plan was simple; Sonya was going to pose as Paris's new client. That way they could meet in public where Derrick would see them and potentially fall for Sonya.

This whole thing was messed up. Paris was well aware that she couldn't have the best of both worlds. The longer she faked romantic feelings for Derrick the more real they became. It no longer mattered to her that he was a married man. As a matter of fact, their rendezvouses were more exciting knowing that Melody could find them at any moment. Being around Sonya was nothing short of annoying. Per Monique's instructions, they went shopping together, grabbed lunch, and sometimes even breakfast, all in a bid for Derrick to see them and hopefully be drawn to Sonya. She was a younger and perkier version of Paris so it was a no-brainer.

"What do you actually do?" Paris asked Sonya. They were at one of the hottest bars in town pretending to enjoy a girl's night out.

"None of your business," Sonya replied cheekily.

"I'm paying you, so it's definitely my business," Paris bit back.

"Whatever," Sonya rolled her eyes. "You're not very smart are you Mrs. Johnson?"

"You listen here-"

"No, you listen bitch," Sonya growled. "Try me and you'll leave here in a body bag. You better ask about me."

Paris chuckled and slammed her glass on the counter. "You don't know who you're dealing with little girl. Sit your ass down and behave before I slice your throat."

Now, Paris was not a violent person, but she knew not to show fear otherwise it would end badly for her. After all, she was a product of the streets. Sonya looked around and slowly returned to her seat and crossed her legs.

"Real recognize real," Sonya said with a smile on her face. "I think

I like you Mrs. Johnson."

"No one will believe we're friends if you keep calling me that. Just call me Paris."

There was no sign of Derrick after almost two hours, so they decided to leave the bar and try the diner. Paris remembered him telling her that he ate there every day. She didn't think he'd be there at night but it was worth a shot.

As luck would have it, Derrick walked in just as Paris was about to pay the bill. He looked as handsome as ever in black jeans and a white V-neck t-shirt. Just the sight of him was enough to intoxicate Paris and make her mind go blank. She cleared her throat and straightened her leather skirt.

Derrick flashed a charming smile and gave the bartender a signal.

"Good evening ladies. May I join you?"

"Hi handsome," Sonya replied seductively.

"Back off, Sonya! He's mine," Paris scowled. This was the plan, but Paris genuinely wanted Sonya to back off.

Derrick chuckled and kissed Paris on the cheek. "It's alright, Sugar, save that fire for later."

Sonya suggested they move to one of the tables, but Derrick led them to the VIP lounge instead. The dimmed lights and purple couches made Paris feel uncomfortable. It looked like a stripper dungeon and smelled like one too.

Derrick sat between them and struck up a conversation with Sonya almost immediately. They were talking and laughing as if they'd known each other for ages. Their comfort around each other made Paris uncomfortable; she felt like a third wheel.

Their bodies were angled towards one another and Sonya kept pressing up against him as if her gigantic fake breasts weren't already visible. This was what Paris originally wanted, but it angered her now that it was happening.

"I need to get going," Paris said out of the blue.

"Okay," Derrick muttered but his eyes were still on Sonya. "Drive safe."

Paris scoffed and stormed out. She dialed Monique's number before she reached her car.

"Hey sis," Monique answered sounding too relaxed.

"Can you believe that bastard ignored me!"

"Isn't that what you wanted? You should be celebrating right now, not throwing a fit."

128

"I'm not throwing a fit, Monique. I just hate being ignored.

"Mm hm."

"Are you even listening to me? What are you doing?" "Releasing some tension," Monique moaned.

"Why would you answer the phone during sex! Ugh, you're disgusting."

Paris ended the call and tried to start her car but it wouldn't turn on. She tried over and over again but got nothing. Calling AAA would be the logical thing to do, but Paris knew that her car had been tampered with. It was either by Derrick or someone else who didn't want her to leave the premises.

She dialed her husband's number immediately and told him where she was and what had happened. Without questioning her, he told her he'd be there in a few minutes and instructed her not to move or touch anything until he arrived.

Maleek's car sped into the parking lot 10 minutes later and he parked in the space right next to her. He jumped out and ran to driver's side the car looking panicked. Paris could see the fear in his eyes and it broke her heart. His cousin had died in a car bombing when he was a teenager, so he freaked out any time she had issues with her car.

"I'm okay, baby," she comforted him when he yanked her door open.

"What if it's a setup, Paris? What if someone is trying to kill you?"

"I… I left my lights on," She lied.

"W-why didn't you tell me that on the phone?" he yelled.

"I'm sorry my love. I panicked because there was some guys looking in my direction."

Maleek hugged her and apologized for yelling. He called AAA to pick the car up and took care of everything else while she sat in his car watching through the rearview mirror.

Tears welled up in her eyes when Derrick emerged from the bar with his arms around Sonya's waist. She wasn't crying because of Derrick, but because seeing him and her husband side by side made her realize how messed up she was.

What she felt was no longer guilt but grief. Maleek was hard at work making sure she was taken care of and yet it still broke her heart that Derrick had left with the woman she had set up for him. This was a new low, even for her.

Maleek returned to the car and asked if she was okay. He

apologized repeatedly for yelling at her earlier, thinking that was the reason for the tears in her eyes when she was crying because Derrick was spending the night with another woman.

"I don't deserve you," she told her husband.

"Baby, all you did was go to a bar," he chuckled. "Don't be so hard on yourself."

"What happened to me, Maleek? When did I become this person?"

"It's probably just a midlife crisis. You'll be alright. I promise."

Maleek took his jacket off and covered her legs with it. He could see how uncomfortable she was in her mini skirt. Because she had been so understanding and forgiving over the years, Maleek settled in his heart that he would do the same for her while she went through her midlife crisis. Up to that point, he had been the one breaking her heart constantly, so he decided to just be there for her and support her through whatever she was going through.

Chapter 15

Maleek walked into the room with a tray in his hands and a bright smile on his face. "A beautiful breakfast for a beautiful lady."

"Pancakes and strawberries are hardly the definition of beauty," she giggled. "They are the height of my skillset in the kitchen, therefore they are classified as beauty."

"I can't argue with that."

He set the tray on her lap and put his palm to her forehead. "Are you feeling any better today?"

"Yeah. I've just been really tired lately. I guess I've taken on too much."

"You can cancel the party if it's too stressful, honey. Your health is more important to me," Maleek said sincerely.

"I'm fine," she insisted. "And there's no way I'm cancelling the party. I've put in a lot of time, money, and energy into this."

"Okay, then at least promise me you will set up a visit with the doctor just to make sure it's nothing more than fatigue."

"I promise. I can't go today, though. We have to finalize the catering and guest list."

Maleek left for work after she promised to make an appointment with their family doctor. It was sweet how worried he was, but she was beginning to feel smothered. It had been two weeks since the bar incident and she hadn't heard from Derrick.

Monique had called to tell her that Sonya had made major progress with him and that they were meeting almost every day. It was a bittersweet feeling, but Monique assured her it was for the best.

Her days went back to being empty and boring, with the exception of the party planning. There was nothing eventful about her life anymore. She assumed that the big mental change was the reason she was getting physically ill. All the anxiety and stress she had been under for months came to an end as suddenly as it had begun so of course, it would affect her physically.

Everyone seemed so preoccupied with their lives that they had no time for her.

Monique was suddenly too busy to meet up with her; the ladies from the church had taken her off all committees because she had neglected her duties for months, and the other mom's from the kids' school excluded her from their gatherings. Everyone just cut her off as though she no longer existed.

She was so desperate for human interaction that against her better judgment she called Derrick- something Monique had warned her against. No one else was willing to meet up with her except for him. What she needed from him was not a sexual relationship, but friendship. She needed a friend.

They met up at the diner as usual, but this time Derrick didn't seem friendly or tolerant. He kept looking at his watch as she spoke and making random noises of approval whenever she asked him a question. Paris sucked in her bottom lip to hide the quivering; she was on the verge of tears.

"Why do you hate me now?" she asked Derrick. "You couldn't get enough of me a few months ago, now you're acting like you'd rather be anywhere else in the world as long as it wasn't here with me."

"Sonya told me everything about the little game you were playing," he said bluntly. "And guess what? It actually happened. I fell for her, so you got what you wanted. Now what more do you want from me?"

She didn't bother apologizing for her deception because she wasn't sorry. "I just need a friend right now, Derrick."

Derrick threw his head back and laughed. His laugh was filled with mockery rather than humor. "I never signed up to be your damn friend, Paris. I wanted one thing only from you, I got it and I have moved on."

"You're lying."

"And you're a delusional woman."

Paris hated losing. She would do anything possible to come out on top, so she quickly got up, sat next to him, and grabbed his crotch. As expected, Derrick stiffened as his manhood stood to attention under the trance her touch.

"I think you're the delusional one," she smirked.

He placed his hand over hers and directed her hand in a circular motion. "I'm glad you know I will always want you. I was willing to let you go, but you came running back to me sugar, so this time we go all the way."

Paris stopped and tried to pull her hand away but he held it in place. "N-No, this is not what I want Derrick."

"Too late," he smiled and planted a soft kiss on her cheek. "Let's get out of here."

"I can't. I've got meetings to attend."

"Fine, but if you don't show up at the hotel at 6 pm, I will come to your house and drag you out myself. Remember, you awoke the sleeping tiger, so now you have to deal with the consequences."

The rest of the day was a blur. Paris couldn't remember which menu she approved or how many people were on the guest list. She felt like crying each time she replayed what Derrick had said to her earlier that day. It was too shameful to admit to Monique that all their hard work had gone to waste because of her impulsive behavior.

She was standing outside the hotel at 5:55 pm willing herself to turn and run, but there was no point because Derrick would find her wherever she went. "This is the last time," she sighed.

To her surprise, Sonya opened the door and greeted her with a sultry smile. "You're right on time."

"What are you doing here?" Paris frowned.

"You'll find out soon enough."

There was something unsettling about the way Sonya looked at her. They always scowled at each other in the past, but now Sonya was looking at her like she wanted to rip her clothes off.

Paris clutched her bag closer to her body and walked into the room to find Derrick lounging on the bed with a towel around his waist. From their past experiences, she deduced that he was naked.

"Why is she here?" Paris asked Derrick.

"For the same reason you're here," Derrick replied. "Now loosen up. We're about to have some fun."

Sonya came up behind her and began to undress her against her will. Derrick ordered her to stay still so she did, even though she felt violated.

"You look much better with your clothes off," Sonya giggled. "I'm going to have so much fun with you."

Regardless of what Paris had done, lesbianism was where she drew the line. It was something she had never even dreamed of trying, and now Derrick was forcing her into it. At this point she shouldn't have been surprised because Derrick kept showing her who he was, she just refused to believe it.

Sonya pushed her on the bed, spread her legs wide, and went down on her while Derrick watched. As much as Paris wanted to fight it, her eyes rolled back in her head and she gave in to the explosion of pleasure. Her mind kept telling her to snap out of it and make Sonya stopped, but her body had other ideas.

After a while, Derrick began to instruct them on what to do with each other while he sat back and watched. It was Paris's first sexual experience with a woman and it far exceeded her expectations. She found it more erotic than her experiences with men because Sonya seemed to understand her body in ways that blew her mind.

Paris was spent after multiple orgasms, but Sonya and Derrick were just getting started. Derrick finally joined them, and it became a three-way encounter. She now knew why men always suggested threesomes. Being pleasured by a man and a woman at the same time was the best thing ever.

"That's right, baby. Don't fight it." Sonya moaned when Paris took charge and copied what Sonya had done to her earlier.

It was after midnight when Derrick allowed Paris to go home. This time she knew Maleek wouldn't let her off the hook. Anyone who had ever had sex before could smell it reeking from her clothing. Still, she prayed he'd let it go or that she would find him asleep.

But of course, nothing was working in her favor lately. Maleek was pacing back and forth when she walked into the house. Judging by the look on his face, she wasn't going to be let off the hook this time around.

"Start talking," he said calmly.

"I went out for a drive to clear my head," she lied effortlessly.

Maleek shook his head and cracked his knuckles. "You take me for a fool."

"What? Are you going to hit me now?" she scoffed.

"What the hell is wrong with you, Paris? I know you're cheating on me!"

"You don't know shit."

"The whole neighborhood can smell you!" he retorted.

"Oh, so it's a crime for a woman to pleasure herself now? I'm not like you, Maleek. I will never be a lowlife cheating asshole like you."

Her words cut him deep. It was written all over his face, but she wasn't going to stick around much longer because she knew she'd end up cracking and exposing herself. What she had said to him was disgusting and uncalled for. If anything, what she was doing was worse than all the affairs he had because his had never involved emotion. He was battling an addiction. It wasn't the same as her emotional connection to Derrick. Maleek had never contemplated leaving her for his mistresses, but she had greatly considered leaving him and their children when she was at the height of her desire for Derrick. She was the lowlife cheating asshole between the two of them, but she would never admit that to him as long as she lived.

Chapter 16

"Therapy is for white people."

These are the words that were occupying Paris's thoughts as she drove aimlessly around the city. She had been doing this all day every day for a week until it was time to pick up the kids. Paris couldn't stand being in the house alone, not to mention the awful smell that she had failed to locate the source of, so she would go out for long drives until it was time to do her motherly duties for the kids or her mistress duties for Derrick.

"Therapy is for white people." She tried to convince herself.

Of course, she was wise enough to know that this wasn't true. After all, she and Maleek had gone for couples counseling and they had a family therapist. But oddly enough, she felt ashamed about it this time around. She felt ashamed to go to someone who had known her family for years and reveal her unfaithfulness to her marriage.

Moreover, Maleek would see the charge on the credit card statement and ask her a ton of questions that she didn't have the strength to deal with. Her mental and emotional capacity was truly spent this time around. Nothing excited her anymore. She didn't feel like cooking, cleaning, working, or even engaging in conversation. All she wanted to do all day was either sleep or drive around the city.

An idea popped into her head and she sped to the nearest ATM to withdraw some cash. "No plastic, no trail," she chuckled as she pulled out the money. She accepted that she needed to talk to someone, but she wasn't dumb enough to leave any evidence behind.

Now that she had a wad of cash, all she needed to do was find a good therapist. Luckily, she had driven around town enough times that she'd spotted a few places that seemed legit. Even if they weren't, she wouldn't mind, just as long as she got to tell someone what a disgusting person she had become.

The quaint redbrick building with the white French doors had an unusual charm to it that drew her in. It stood out from all the other buildings like an exposed secret. Well, her logic was flawed, but she was running with it anyway.

Right on brand, a charming receptionist greeted her with a

beautiful smile. "Good morning ma'am! Do you have an appointment?"

"Uh, well no, actually."

"You're in luck! Dr. Javier is free all morning. Please fill this form in the meantime while I check to see if the doctor can see you now."

Paris thanked her and sat down to fill out the standard form. For a second, she considered giving fake information, but the thought of lying about something else made her sick to her stomach. She didn't want to be a liar anymore.

The receptionist returned with the same sickly sweet smile on her face as before. "Right this way, ma'am. He'll see you now."

Paris felt like she was being led to the slaughterhouse even though the hallway was brightly lit. Dr. Javier's office wasn't any better. Although the earthy tones of the room were pretty standard, Paris felt suffocated.

"Please take a seat," Dr. Javier said in a soothing voice. He was a slightly overweight man in his mid-forties wearing oversized pants, but he had a calming presence about him that put her mind at ease.

"I'm a bad person," she blurted out before he could ask her anything. "I've been cheating on my husband for months. Well, to be fair, he's been cheating on me for years, but that's not the point."

"So you wanted revenge?"

"No… yes! I was fed up and wanted to give him a taste of his own medicine but once I started I couldn't stop. This man is so addicting. No matter how many times I wanted to stop, I just couldn't. I kept going back over and over again and now I can't stop even if I wanted to because he's threatening me."

"Ms. Johnson, I can tell that you're a good woman. You walked into my office today because the guilt has been eating you up and you had to talk to someone. How accurate is this?"

"More than I can express," she sniffled.

"Exactly. You've made a few mistakes, and that's okay. Making mistakes is part of the human experience. I don't know your husband, but I think he will forgive you if you have an honest conversation with him."

"But I've developed feelings for this other guy," she sobbed. "I'm sorry; I don't know why I'm crying. I've been so emotional lately."

"It's okay to cry; you're overwhelmed. That feeling of relief after a good cry will be multiplied when you come clean to your husband. The emotional attachment you've developed for this other man is also normal, but I doubt you want to leave your husband for him because you would have done it already if you cared about him that much."

"I do love him. I love Maleek so much, that's why this is killing me inside. I feel like there's no way out. This other man makes me feel desirable. When I'm with him I feel like a woman."

"Is feeling desirable worth losing your family? Ms. Johnson, I can't tell you what to do, but I can tell you that some things are just not worth it. You cannot rely on someone else to make you feel sexy or desirable. That's a different conversation."

Paris mulled over Dr. Javier's words for the rest of the day. He was right. Ever since she met Derrick, she had become selfish. Feeling sexy had never been a problem for her, so why did she use it as an excuse to justify her infidelity?

Derrick: Same time. Same place. Don't be late.

She slammed her head back on the headrest over and over until it hurt. It wasn't guilt that spurred this on, but rather hate. Paris hated herself for the excitement that rushed through her body when she received his text. The excitement that Sonya would be involved again.

Not knowing what else to do, she called Monique and asked her to pick the kids up from school and cover for her with Maleek. And like the good friend that she was, Monique agreed without hesitation.

Having cheated many times before, Paris knew to always be

prepared. She had a bag in the trunk filled with everything she needed to spruce up whenever he called for her. Yes, it was shameful, she knew that, but she couldn't help it. Lingerie, sexy dresses, 6-inch heels; she had it all ready and waiting to be used.

This time she was going for a dangerous look with her black lace lingerie and bold red lipstick. She covered up with a black coat and finished her look with fire-red heels. The hotel employees no longer paid attention when she walked in because they knew what she was there to do. It was shameful, but she was already in too deep.

"Hey sexy," she smiled when Derrick opened the door shirtless. "I see you came ready," he smirked.

Something felt off when she walked into the room. She hadn't noticed anyone else in the room, but it still felt different. She spun around to make Derrick aware of the uneasiness that she was feeling but instead came face to face with a man she had never seen before. Her breath hitched in her throat when she glanced down and saw his penis standing to attention.

She folded her arms tightly as though that would protect her. "W-what's going on, Derrick? Who is this?"

"Cut the act, Sugar," Derrick said calmly while pouring himself a drink. "That's Joe."

Paris began to panic when she realized what was about to happen. "But what about Sonya? No, not even that. Derrick, I didn't agree to this."

"Don't make me angry, Sugar," he said in a sing-song manner.

"No, Derrick! I'm not doing this. I'm leaving."

Derrick made a weird grunting noise that she had never heard before but it seemed to make sense to Joe because he sprang into action. Before she could process what was happening, Joe had ripped her coat off and tossed her onto the bed.

A single tear rolled down her face when Joe entered her. Her body went limp and she just lay there as he rammed into her repeatedly while Derrick watched. As if that were not enough, Derrick instructed Joe to flip her over so he could join and they both went at it like animals with no regard for her body or her feelings.

She cried silently and prayed that it would end soon. At that point, she would give anything to be back home in her warm bed with her husband by her side. The emotional connection she believed she had with Derrick died instantly. He was a beast. A sick twisted beast who had no regard for her body or her heart.

When Derrick realized that she was crying he grabbed her by the hair and slapped her repeatedly while yelling, "Shut the fuck up and suck my dick or I will slit your throat, bitch!" while shoving his penis in her face.

If there was a list of times she felt violated, this one would take the top spot. A random man she didn't know was grunting and sweating all over her while he inserted his penis inside of her, and the man she thought she had feelings for was choking her with his. Even though Derrick had violated her before, she never thought it would come to this. This was too much.

They pushed her off the bed when they were done and she landed knees-first on the floor. Nothing about what had just happened was normal or respectful. To make matters worse, they began to discuss her "performance" as though she weren't there.

The more they talked Paris realized that she was dealing with something far more sinister than she could even imagine. Derrick spoke like he did this for a living. Everything he said came out comfortable and natural as though he was ordering a meal at a restaurant.

She crawled out of the room with her coat barely covering her naked body. There was no one to turn to anymore. No scheming would get her out of this. Derrick was either a pimp or a really sick man. But first, she had to get to the hospital and get herself checked because neither Joe nor Derrick had used protection.

Chapter 17

"Congratulations, Mrs. Johnson, you're four weeks pregnant," the doctor told her.

Paris burst out laughing. "Don't play like that Doctor . Trust me, there's no way I'm pregnant."

The doctor turned to the nurse and asked about her facial bruises, after which he suggested they take her in for a CT scan. Paris's laughter died out when she saw the file in the doctor's hand.

"You don't understand. I can't get pregnant! Listen to me, my husband had a vastectomy, I can't get pregnant." She said hysterically.

"Calm down, ma'am. Stress is not good for the baby," the doctor said. But Paris wasn't having it. The last thing Paris remembered was hyperventilating and a needle being stuck in her arm.

The smiling face of an elderly nurse was the first thing she saw when she woke up a few hours later. For some reason, the nurse was just sitting there humming amazing grace.

"How are you feeling, dear?" the nurse asked Paris.

Paris's eyes welled up with tears again. "I want to die."

"I don't know what you're going through, but I'm telling you right now that this too shall pass. The baby growing in your womb is a blessing."

"I thought that was a dream" Paris sighed and blew her nose. "I wish this was all a dream."

"You're going to be alright, dear. I know it's hard, but stay strong and keep fighting. Don't give up."

The nurse got up and left after giving Paris a warm hug. Her presence alone was proof that kindness still existed in the world. That gesture comforted her more than she could express. It's like she knew that Paris was contemplating suicide once again. It felt like the easy way out.

With the recent turn of events, it was evident that lying was no longer an option. She had to tell Maleek the truth. It would be far better if it came from her than from someone else who could spin the narrative.

As if he knew she was thinking about him, Maleek came running into the room in a panic. He was firing so many questions at her; questions she didn't want to answer in a hospital room. Maleek was infuriated when he saw the bruises on her face. As usual, he made assumptions about what had happened instead of letting her speak. This was beneficial in the past because it got her off the hook whenever she couldn't come up with a lie, but this time she was ready to air it all out.

Paris gently touched her husband's arm to get him to settle down. He took her signal and sat beside her, but she could feel his body trembling from the anger. She could have easily gone with his theory about someone jumping her, but she was done with the lies. Maleek was going to hear the truth from her mouth.

"Please take me home," she croaked. Her voice was hoarse from all the crying she had done.

"Okay, my love, but at least tell me what happened. Who did this to you?"

"I'll tell you everything at home. I promise."

What was so great about Maleek was that he knew when to give her space. He wasn't someone who hovered when she asked for time to think or when she just needed to be alone. He truly was a great husband. More than anything, she wished she had never taken him for granted. It was hard to believe that she had once compared him to Derrick.

Maleek snuck glances at her as he drove. It was plain to see the worry in his eyes. Most people would be dying of curiosity, but he was only worried about her being okay. The bruises on her face bothered him without a doubt, but he put her feelings first and kept his mouth shut.

The ride felt shorter than Paris would have preferred. But no amount of time would reduce the pain she was about to inflict on her husband's heart. Like a true gentleman, he helped her out of the car and informed her that he had organized for her car to be driven back to the house so she wouldn't worry.

When she heard this she couldn't contain her tears anymore. She let out an ear- splitting wail and clutched onto her husband. The agony she felt could not be expressed with words. She loathed herself for putting her selfish desires first because it wasn't even worth it. Having multiple orgasms was never worth losing the love of her life.

Maleek scooped her into his arms and took her up to their room. She heard the kids asking if she was alright and Maleek telling them to give her some space, which only made her cry harder. This she couldn't blame on pregnancy hormones.

Paris cried until her tears ran dry and were replaced with hiccups. Before Maleek left the house she heard the kids complaining about going to so many sleepovers. She didn't even realize that the year had gone by with her barely spending time with her children because she had been shipping them off to different people's homes almost every weekend just so she could have uninterrupted sex with a man who wasn't their father.

It was as though she had been living in darkness and suddenly the lights were switched on. The results of her selfish actions were all around her. Every bad decision she had made since she met Derrick had indirectly hurt those she loved most even when she wasn't aware of it.

"I brought pizza!" Maleek yelled out when he walked into the room an hour later. "I got you wings as well. I went to that little place on the corner of Mason and Green that you love you much. And of course I didn't forget desert…"

"I'm pregnant," Paris blurted out. She wanted to tell him about the affair first, but all the food he'd brought into the room was so nauseating that she couldn't focus.

Maleek sprang into action and quickly threw the bags of food down the stairs before returning to the room. What confused her was the huge smile he had on his face. He began to pace back and forth while mumbling about a dream he had. She was now more puzzled than afraid.

"You're making me dizzy," she told him. "What are you

mumbling about?"

"I had this crazy dream the other night! I thought I was just going crazy but it turns out God was trying to tell me we were blessed with another child. I even did some research and it turns out a vasectomy can be reversed naturally."

"But... how?"

"The human body is crazy, baby," he laughed. "I can't believe this is happening!"

His excitement was even more heartbreaking because even if his body had miraculously reversed the vasectomy, he still wasn't the father. The doctor told her she was four weeks along, which meant there was no way it could have been Maleek's baby.

They weren't having sex that often. Sometimes they'd go two weeks without doing it, and it so happened that one of their droughts happened five weeks ago. They had gone almost three weeks without sex, but in that time she had been with Derrick a total of seven times.

Maleek was so over the moon that he went to get checked the very next morning, and as if someone was playing a sick joke on them, his vasectomy had indeed been reversed. The doctor explained that it was rare but not impossible, and Maleek was one of the "lucky ones".

What most people didn't know was that Maleek had always wanted more children but settled on two because Paris didn't want any more. She wanted to give their two kids the best life possible. Their families constantly pressured them to have more kids for years, but Maleek told them a fake story about him becoming impotent due to an accident at work. They both knew that their families would give them hell if they found out about the vasectomy.

The real reason why Maleek opted for the vasectomy was that Paris's body rejected every form of contraceptive she was given. It was after her third visit to the ER that Maleek offered to get a vasectomy instead. They chose to keep this a secret from everyone so that they wouldn't give Paris a hard time.

Listening to Maleek ramble about all the things he wants to purchase for the baby only made her want to tell him the truth sooner. She made a promise to herself to come clean and live an honest life going forward, and that's exactly what she was going to do.

"Maleek, please stop."

"Oh! I'm sorry. I'll just toss this out," he said halfway to the bin to dump the lasagna he had just made.

"No, no, it's not that. I need to tell you something."

Maleek put the lasagna back in the oven and joined her on the couch. He looked at her expectantly, as though she'd give him even more "good news" but this time it was the opposite. This time she was going to break his heart.

"What is it, honey?" he rubbed her leg lovingly.

She took a deep breath and said, "Maleek, this isn't your baby."

"Stop playing," he chuckled. "You've never been a good liar."

"I'm serious this time. This is not your baby."

Maleek pulled his hand away before she could touch it and crossed his arms. He didn't yell or throw a fit. He just sat there with a deep frown on his face staring at the wall. His silence made her nervous.

"You cheated on me," he laughed humorlessly. "Is it someone I know?"

"You don't know him, but you've met him," she answered truthfully.

Maleek cursed under his breath but maintained his composure. "I guess this is what it feels like."

"I'm so sorry, my love. I'll tell you everything."

"I don't want to know," he said with finality and got up to leave.

"Maleek, please! You need to know. I can't live with this anymore," she pleaded.

He wouldn't turn around to face her, but he decided to hear her out. "Tell me every damn thing, and don't lie to me again."

Chapter 18

Paris told Maleek everything. She told him every little detail from how she met Derrick down to when, where, and how they had sex. It was the most painful conversation she'd ever had in life. Maleek sat quietly the whole time, with the only sound coming from him being sniffles.

They were both in tears as Paris explained how she felt and why she kept going back.

Each word was like a dagger to Maleek's heart but he stayed silent and allowed her to get everything off her chest.

"Maleek, I love you. I know that sounds like a lie but I mean it with everything in me."

"Was this about revenge?" he asked her, still unable to look at her. "I know I cheated for years, but I never built an emotional connection with anyone. I never even imagined leaving you for another woman."

"I know, baby, I know," she sobbed. "I was selfish."

"Was it about revenge?" he asked again.

"The first time? Yes. But after that it was pure selfishness. I was driven by lust and--"

"So you're attracted to him?" Maleek cut her off. "All those times you were not in the mood to have sex with me was because you'd been with him? What was all that shit Monique told me? Is there even a surprise party?"

"Yes! The party is real and it is happening. Maleek, I told you everything. I've answered all your questions. Please yell at me or hit me, or divorce me if you have to, but I cannot answer the same questions again."

"You're the one who messed up here. You're not going to play the victim." He huffed.

"That's not what I'm doing."

"Then why are you crying?" he challenged.

"Because I'm pregnant, you idiot! I had an affair and hurt the person I love more than anything! I've been violated and humiliated; I live in fear; and I tried to drive off a bridge twice. I hate myself right now, but being honest with you was way more important than anything I feel."

Maleek sighed and plopped back on the couch. He looked as defeated as she felt. Just the thought of his wife naked with another man made him want to kill the bastard, but he also accepted that he was the root cause of both their affairs.

He thought back to the first time Paris found out he had cheated on her. The pain and betrayal were evident in her eyes, but she didn't leave him even though she had every reason to. What she did was assure him that she loved him, which was followed by a threat to castrate him if he ever did it again.

The next time, she caught him red-handed. He lied about working late so she brought him dinner at the office and found him and his secretary naked on his desk. She yelled and cried, but the next morning she had breakfast ready for him and told him she wasn't going to forgive him again.

And what did she do all the years since? She forgave him. As much as it hurt her each time he betrayed her trust, she put her feelings aside and offered forgiveness. They had been together for over two decades, and this was the first time she had ever done anything that truly cut him deep.

"Did it take you so long to come clean because you thought I'd leave you?" he asked her after what felt like an eternity of silence.

"Yes," she nodded. "But I really didn't want to hurt you. In trying not to hurt you I got myself entangled with someone dangerous."

"I don't think he'll hurt you, sweetheart. I know he's a cop but he's not above the law," Maleek reasoned.

"No, honey, I think he's much more powerful than we think. After this last time I feel like he could be a pimp or something."

"Listen, Paris, I don't care who that bastard thinks he is, but I won't let him hurt you. I've got you, okay?"

She bit her quivering lip to stop the tears but it was pointless. "What about the baby?" "This baby is a part of you, so I will love him or her as my own," he assured her.

"Am I dreaming? How are you so calm and accepting of all this?"

"Paris, you've stood by me through everything. If you could forgive me for betraying you countless times then I can forgive you for this. I love you, honey. Just promise you will never hide anything from me from now on."

Maleek spent the rest of the day pampering Paris, which wasn't how she pictured the day going. Now she understood why her mother always spoke about forgiveness. Being on the receiving end of it was one of the greatest blessings she had ever received.

Peace had been the missing piece in their lives, and now that everything was out in the open it felt like nothing could shake them. Granted they needed couples therapy again, but it was a small price to pay for peace.

It was almost as if Derrick knew that she and Maleek had reconciled because he didn't bother her for a couple of days. She didn't want to jinx anything or awaken the sleeping beast, but she knew him well enough to know that he had something up his sleeve. The curiosity was eating her up, and funny enough, Maleek felt the same way.

Derrick was a predator. He knew exactly when to lay low and when to strike, but this time she wanted to strike first, so instead of waiting for him to call her, she decided to pay him a visit at the hotel first.

Maleek was on standby in the car in case things got out of hand. The plan was to find evidence of Derrick's shady behavior or get him to talk about it. Her phone was connected on the line with Maleek and he was recording the whole thing from the car.

She was given the room key without being questioned because she "visited" so frequently, and luckily the room was empty. Well, it had traces of Derrick everywhere, but no one was there. Paris immediately got to work rummaging through drawers for anything incriminating and looking in every corner for a hidden camera.

"Bingo!" she exclaimed when she found the camera in an inconspicuous plant. She pulled it out and crushed it with her boot.

Before she could continue her search she heard Derrick's voice outside the door so she ran and hid behind the thick velvet curtain. Derrick never opened the curtains so there was no chance he'd find her. She could only hope he wasn't there with another woman because she'd be stuck there for hours if that was the case.

"You better fix this, Tony! There will be hell to pay if I lose this client." He growled at the person on the other end of the line.

Paris could only hear Derrick's side of the conversation, and from what she had gathered he wasn't just a pimp but a drug lord. It seemed like he was the boss because he was now on his third call and each person he spoke to seemed to be deathly afraid of him.

"Yo, Damar, how's it going with the Italian client?" Derrick spoke calmly on his fourth call.

"Yes, of course he'll love her. I tested her out for months and I think she's perfect. I'm telling you man, she's the total package; the ass, the tits, the itty bitty waist."

Paris prayed that he wasn't talking about her. Although she matched the description he had given, she could think of one other person who did as well and that was Sonya. She felt nauseous at the thought of putting an innocent woman's life in danger.

"Listen," Derrick continued. "I think she could go for much higher. Get him up to a million. Once he agrees, I'll have her on the next flight to Italy. Trust me, Sugar is a seasoned woman with a tight pussy; she can sell for much higher."

Paris audibly gasped and quickly covered her mouth with her hand when she realized that Derrick had stopped talking. It was as if the room was vacant once again, but she knew he was there still there. Her heart dropped when she felt something press against her chest.

There was no doubt in her mind that it was a gun.

"Come out or say your last words," Derrick said menacingly.

She slowly moved the curtain and came face to face with the steel-faced man holding a gun. He squinted his eyes and flexed his jaw, which meant he was furious. She had to think quickly to diffuse the situation otherwise Maleek would probably call the cops, which she didn't want.

"You know how I feel about disrespect," he said in a low voice. "For a split second I considered sending you away in business class because you've been so good, but you've blown it, Sugar."

It was only then that it hit her in the face. "Oh my god, you're a human trafficker," she said breathlessly.

"Yes, and you're next to go, Sugar."

"My name is Paris," she gritted her teeth.

"Not anymore, Sugar," he said nonchalantly. "I hope you said goodbye to that husband of yours because the next place you're going to be is in a suitcase to Italy."

There was only one way out of this situation. She swore she wouldn't say anything, but it was her only lifeline, and she was grateful for it.

"I'm pregnant," she said confidently. "Tell me, Derrick, are you going to sell off the mother of your unborn child?"

Chapter 19

"You're lying," Derrick insisted.

"I'm five weeks along now. I went to the hospital right after you forced me to have sex with you and Joe because neither of you used protection; that's how I found out."

It was like a switch went on the moment she explained. He immediately dialed Damar's number and told him to call off the sale with the Italian client. It seemed as though Damar argued this instruction and demanded an explanation because Derrick suddenly yelled at him to remind him who the boss was between the both of them and ended the call.

"I'm going to be a father," Derrick mumbled in shock. It looked like he was experiencing a wave of varying emotions.

"Look, Derrick. You and I had a good run and it was fun while it lasted, but this is where it ends. I didn't expect to get pregnant again but it happened. I need to stop all the games and focus on being a mom."

"I agree," he replied thoughtfully. "We'll need a buy a house with at least four bedrooms in case we have more kids and—"

"Whoa! Whoa! Whoa! I'm not moving in with you," she interrupted before he got carried away.

Derrick stared at her blankly for a few seconds. She could see that he was struggling to process what she had just said.

"I'm not leaving my family," she clarified. "Maleek and I are going to raise this baby."

"But it's my baby…"

"I know, but all you've done is threaten and abuse me. How can we raise a child together?"

"That was business, this is personal," he said as though it was the most logical explanation.

The door suddenly swung open and there stood Maleek fuming.

"Step away from my wife," he barked.

Derrick looked confused, and for the first time caught off guard. When it finally clicked that Paris had told her husband the truth, Derrick's face contorted back to the evil scowl she had become accustomed to.

"I'll kill both of you," he said menacingly.

Paris ran to Maleek and stood behind him, beckoning him to leave but he wouldn't budge. Now that she knew who Derrick was and the business he was in, she was afraid for their lives, but Maleek wasn't fazed. Maleek cracked his knuckles and flexed his shoulders.

"You're not wrong," he said calmly. "I have no doubt you can kill the both of us right here right now. But before you do anything crazy, it would interest you to know that everything that has been said from the second my wife walked into this room is being recorded."

"You're bluffing," Derrick countered immediately.

"I could be," Maleek chuckled. "But if I'm not, and you do indeed kill us then you, Captain Derrick Brown, will definitely rot in prison."

"The recording won't be leaked if I kill you," Derrick reasoned.

"Smart man! That's why this is being streamed right now. Someone in an unknown location has been listening in this whole time and will release it if my wife and I don't walk out of here within the next 5 minutes."

Derrick threw his head back and let out a boisterous laugh. "Go ahead and send it to the police! It'll disappear before the file is even opened."

"Who said anything about the police? My connections will release this straight to the media. We all know you can't fight the media."

Maleek and Paris walked out of the hotel hand-in-hand a few minutes later. Paris couldn't believe how intelligent and brave her husband had been in that situation. She had never seen this side of him before and she found it extremely sexy.

"Was it really being streamed?" she asked him once they were in the confines of their vehicle.

"Of course," he said proudly. "I had a hunch that this guy was into some shady dealings so I contacted one of my friends in IT and we set this whole thing up."

Maleek went on to explain that his friend was not only one of the top IT experts in the country but also a very talented hacker. The plan they'd come up with was to hack into major news stations and release Derrick's recording live during the evening news. Apparently, the guy owed Maleek big time so he was willing to do anything to help him out.

The rest of the ride was silent as they both got lost in their thoughts. Maleek was proud that he had successfully protected his family, and Paris on the other hand, was grateful that they could put everything behind them and enjoy the rest of their lives.

"What is she doing here?" Maleek said. He sounded very irritated.

Paris followed his line of sight until she saw Monique. It was strange that she just showed up without calling first; not that she had to, but she always did anyway. Paris looked back at her husband who looked disgusted by Monique's presence.

"I don't want her in my house," he said sternly. "Why? Did she say something crazy again?"

Maleek didn't bother responding. He parked the car and hopped out without saying another word. Just when Paris thought things had gone back to normal, now she had to mediate between her husband and her best friend. Monique could get very brash with her words sometimes, so there was no doubt she had offended Maleek somehow.

Paris joined Monique on the front step and asked her friend if she was alright. Normally, it would have been Monique asking all the questions, but she seemed very troubled; almost as if someone was chasing her.

"Are you still seeing Derrick?" Monique asked out of the blue.

Paris did a double-take and pursed her lips. "Why are you asking about Derrick all of a sudden? Maleek handled that."

"So you and Maleek aren't getting a divorce then?"

"Monique, what is wrong with you? Why are you asking me this?"

"I think you're making a big mistake," Monique said nervously. "Babe, I have never seen you as happy as you were when you met Derrick. You became a brand new woman; a confident woman with a backbone. You deserve to be the best version of yourself and I think that's with Derrick."

Paris stood up and looked down at the person who had known her for over twenty years. Not once had she ever doubted Monique's friendship or loyalty until that very moment. Something was fishy, but Paris didn't care to find out.

"I think you should leave before I say something we will both regret," Paris said stoically

"I'm just looking out for you, Paris."

"Get off my property before I lose my tempter, Monique. I won't repeat myself."

Paris turned and walked away; leaving her so-called best friend behind. She couldn't believe that Monique of all people tried to convince her to go back to a man who had threatened and abused her. It was like a kick to the gut, but Paris refused to dwell on it or allow it to alter her mood. She should have been celebrating her freedom from Derrick's claws but instead, she felt exhausted and depressed.

The next morning felt just as gloomy as the night before. Paris awakened to a text from none other than Melody herself demanding a meeting to discuss the pregnancy. Peace eluded her ever since she got entangled with Derrick.

Having learned her lesson, Paris immediately showed Maleek the text message and it infuriated him. He too was fed up with the situation and wanted it to just go away. One would think they would back off after being threatened with the recording, but they just kept coming back like addicts.

"Now I don't feel comfortable leaving you here alone all day," Maleek grumbled. "What the hell is wrong with these people? Do we have to move to another city for them to leave us alone?"

"I'm sorry, honey. I wish I had never started all this in the first place." She said sadly. "You don't have to apologize every day, my love. I'm just pissed that these people won't leave us alone. You know what? I'm going to call in sick."

"What should I do about Melody?" she asked.

"Just ignore her. You've been through a lot lately, plus there's this whole party thing happening this weekend. You deserve a day off from all this crap."

Maleek asked his boss if he could work from home for the rest of the week because his pregnant wife needed someone around to help her, and his boss gladly agreed. He had been making a lot of sacrifices ever since she told him the truth and it was beginning to weigh down on him. Without a doubt, it would be selfish to talk to Paris about how he felt because she had always made sacrifices for him when his infidelities were brought to light, but this was different. In this case, their lives were threatened. They had children to worry about as well.

And now, as if life wasn't complicated enough as it was, Monique was pressuring him again and he didn't know what to do.

Chapter 20

The party was spectacular. All their family and friends were in attendance, which made it even more special. Paris and Monique shared a laugh when Maleek walked in and pretended to be shocked. After all, it was meant to be a surprise party. But what was hilarious was Maleek's exaggerated acting.

First, his eyes widened, then he looked around the room, and then came the repeated "Get outta here!" which sounded forced. The guests bought his charade though. Since Maleek had never had a surprise party before no one had a blueprint of his natural reaction to such an event.

"Do you think they bought it?" Maleek asked when he approached them.

"I think you did an excellent job," Monique replied with a bright smile that Paris found to be irritating.

Truthfully speaking, they hadn't really made up yet. They would usually sweep small issues under the rug and just carry on being goofballs together, but this time Paris was truly hurt and offended. What Monique had said to her was not something she could easily gloss over because it wasn't a small matter. Now here Monique stood, smiling brightly at Maleek as if she hadn't said anything malicious a few days prior.

Paris shot her friend a dirty look before intertwining her fingers with her husband and walking off to have some privacy.

"You still haven't told me what Monique said to you that day," Maleek said once they found a quiet corner. Everyone was having a good time so no one noticed that the two of them had snuck off into a quiet corner by themselves.

"I'll tell you about it tomorrow. I just want to enjoy this moment with you."

Maleek took the hint and snaked his arms around her waist pulling her closer until their lips were only an inch apart. "I can't wait to enjoy a little private dessert later."

He went in for a slow and gentle kiss that left her craving for more. Whether Maleek got sexier or the pregnancy hormones were getting stronger, either way, she wanted him to take her down right then and there.

Their steamy kiss was interrupted by someone calling for everyone's attention. They separated and turned to face the stage where Monique stood with a glass of champagne in her hand.

"What in the entire hell is she doing?" Paris asked her husband in an accusatory tone. "Did you ask her to do this?"

"This is a 'surprise party,' babe. How would I ask someone to give a speech at a party I wasn't supposed to know about?"

Paris clenched her fist and gave Monique a piercing side eye along with her full attention. She didn't like this new side of her friend. Again, it could have just been the pregnancy hormones, but her gut was telling her that Monique was up to no good.

"Hi everyone," Monique said cheerfully. "I'm sure most of you know me, and if by the off chance that you don't, turn to your neighbor and asked about me."

Everyone laughed like she'd told the funniest joke.

"I won't take up much of your time," she went on. "I just want to thank you all for coming today to celebrate Maleek, whom we all love so dearly. Y'all know how difficult it is to surprise this man, but we pulled it off!"

At this point, Paris was fuming. Monique was up there giving a speech as though she was Maleek's wife and the mastermind behind the whole celebration. People laughed and cheered as she spoke, but a few family members turned to look at Paris with confused expressions. Surely they too were as shocked as Paris was about what Monique was doing.

"...Thank you all once again. We really appreciate your presence. But before I let you get back to enjoying yourselves, I want us all to raise a congratulatory glass and toast to our friend who recently found out she is expecting! To Paris!"

Gasps and cheers rippled through the room and before Paris could process what Monique had just done, she was surrounded by a sea of people hugging and kissing her. Maleek tried to stay by her side but he was somehow pushed away by the throng of people trying to touch her belly- that wasn't even protruding yet.

After what seemed like an eternity of hugs and uncomfortable conversations, Paris finally managed to slip away to gather herself. One thing she absolutely despised was being the center of attention, and Monique knew that.

Any doubts Paris had about her friend were erased. It was clear as day that this was sabotage. Monique was not in her corner anymore. But even though it hurt, she wanted more than anything to find out the reason why than dwell on the deeds that had been done.

She went in search of her husband because she needed the support and spotted him standing in the same corner as before, but Monique was with him this time. A stranger would have easily mistaken them for a couple judging by the way Monique was hanging onto Maleek's arm as they spoke.

Paris marched up to them and slapped Monique across the face.

"How dare you," she seethed.

"Touch me again Bitch and I'll kick your ass," Monique retaliated.

A few people were starting to pay attention to them so Maleek grabbed Monique by the arm and told her to leave. She tried to protest but he wasn't having it. The more she struggled, the more attention it garnered so Maleek let her go and politely asked her to leave.

"I told you, baby," she said to Maleek. "If I can't have you then no one will."

"Monique, get out of here," Maleek said under his breath.

"Oh my," she giggled. "Didn't you tell wifey dearest that you've been fucking me for years? Oops! Cats out the bag. Let's see if she will be as 'forgiving' as you have claimed she was. You and I are made for each other, Maleek. I'll give you one more chance to divorce this hoe, or else."

"Is she telling the truth?" Paris asked her husband. "Maleek, you've been having sex with my best friend?"

"Paris, baby, please let me explain," he begged.

Paris took a deep breath and shook her head. "I'm not doing this here. I'm going home."

She spun on her heel and headed for the exit. Everything suddenly became meaningless. The marriage she had fought so hard to keep was nothing but a sick joke. There was no point in pretending that love was enough because it wasn't. Love was not the only component to a healthy and happy marriage. What about trust? Loyalty? Respect? Honesty? These were all things that she and Maleek no longer had, so why were they still married?

Paris felt like bursting into tears when she got to the parking lot and found Melody waiting for her. At this point, it felt like she was stuck in a nightmare. There was no way one person could face trouble after trouble without catching a break.

"You've been ignoring me," Melody said plainly. "I hate it when people ignore me."

"Yes, Melody, I'm pregnant with your husband's baby. Now please get out of my way."

Melody didn't even flinch when Paris got in her face and demanded that she step aside. From up close Melody was even more beautiful. Her facial features made her look sweet and innocent, but Paris knew that she was anything but that.

"I always knew my husband was too weak to run the business," Melody wrinkled her nose in disgust. "That pervert is too focused on testing out the product instead of actually delivering."

"Women are not products!" Paris yelled. "You're a sick, sick, woman. How can you sleep at night knowing that you're selling off people into the dangers of sex trafficking?"

"Sweetheart, in life you are either the prey or you are the predator. I prefer to be in control," she shrugged.

"Look, Maleek and I promised that we'd keep our mouths shut as long as you leave our family alone. So please, just leave us alone. I beg you."

Melody put her hand to her chin as though she were seriously considering it, but the glint in her eye said otherwise. Even a blind man could see that she enjoyed instilling fear in people; she fed off of it.

"You know what? I don't think I have it in me to hurt a pregnant woman."

Paris closed her eyes and breathed a sigh of relief thinking the nightmare was over. "Thank you, Melody. Can we please put this behind us now and move on? I swear I'll stay far away from you and your husband from now on."

"Oh, no, no, sweetheart, I think you've misunderstood me," Melody gasped. "What I meant is, I won't hurt you until I rip that thing out of you."

Paris tried to scream but nothing came out. She took a few steps back to put a bit of distance between herself and Melody but she bumped into a very large, mean-looking man, after her second step. It became very clear what was about to happen. Melody's words only confirmed what Paris already knew.

"Did you seriously think I would let that bastard growing inside you derail my business?" she closed the gap and whispered in Paris's ear, "I always deliver," and then the burly man knocked Paris out cold.

Epilogue

Small, dark spaces were near the top of the list of things Paris hated. Her head was throbbing and the air felt thin. She peeled her eyes open and was greeted by complete darkness. From all the possibilities she came up with, the only logical answer was that she was in the trunk of a car.

It wasn't a smooth ride in the least and it didn't help that she was laying on her side. Judging by the numbness in her leg, she had been in that position for a while, which meant wherever they were taking her was definitely out of the city.

There wasn't much space to move around, but she slowly twisted her body until she was lying on her back. No doubt her phone had been taken from her, but she still patted her pockets just in case.

After coming up empty, as expected, she relaxed and closed her eyes. This helped her focus on the sounds around her. She remembered watching a movie in which the person was in a similar situation as she was in, and they were able to deduce their location by paying attention to the feel of the wheels and listening for other sounds as clues.

Paris steadied her breathing and cleared her mind using the techniques she learned from her yoga class. Once she was calm, she was able to feel that they were on a dirt road so she took a wild guess that they someone on the outskirts of the city. To support her hypothesis, the smell of dust infiltrated the boot and assaulted her nostrils. Being pregnant came in handy because her senses were heightened.

When the smell of dust settled, she suddenly picked up a rich floral scent. The smell was comforting because it was familiar. Maleek had a habit of buying her a bouquet of different flowers every week thus she had become accustomed to the different scents.

"Gardenias," she mumbled.

One important thing she had learned from all the crime shows Maleek loved watching was to stay calm and pay attention to your environment, so she did just that. So far she had two clues: the first was they were on a dirt road; and the second was that the place was populated by gardenias because the smell was overwhelming.

Paris relaxed her shoulders and closed her eyes when she heard a door slam and footsteps approaching. An influx of light filled the trunk, but she concentrated and managed to not flinch until someone poked her side with something hard.

An Oscar-worthy performance was the only way to describe Paris's acting. She groaned and peeled her eyes open in a dramatic fashion while touching her head and flinching. After all, she had been hit on the head and kidnapped.

"Get out princess," a mean-looking man said in a gruff voice.

"Where am I?" Paris asked.

"The shop," he answered and then nudged her again with what she now saw was a pistol.

The man helped her out of the trunk and steadied her when she wobbled a little. What he had referred to as "the shop" looked like a vehicle manufacturing factory. He instructed Paris to walk calmly and not do anything stupid otherwise he'd have to kill a couple of people, and she didn't doubt he would, so she followed his orders.

He led her to a hidden side entrance that you wouldn't know was there unless someone showed you. They walked down two flights of stairs into what seemed like a prison. There were rows of small rooms closed off by large steel gates.

Paris folded her lips to prevent the sob that threatened to escape as they walked down the hall to wherever she was being taken. In each of the cells were women of different ages, body types, and ethnicities; each one looking as frightened as the other. Only then did it finally hit her that she was being trafficked.

Discussion Questions

1. Which of these do you think is worse: Emotional or Physical infidelity?

2. Do you think it is okay to cheat if your partner cheated first?

3. How do you feel about your partner having sexual fantasies of someone else?

4. Some people say that cheating is a deal-breaker, but most people stay with an unfaithful partner because of children, finances, or fear. What are your thoughts on this?

5. Do you think you can forgive and move on if your partner cheated on you?

6. What do you think is the best way to heal from infidelity and why?

7. Is Paris justified in her decision to cheat?

www.ingramcontent.com/pod-product-compliance
Lightning Source LLC
Chambersburg PA
CBHW070515260626
47161CB00004B/1558